Praise for R. C. House's
Trackdown at Immigrant Lake

"Marshal Cole Ryerson is cast in the mold of John Wayne's Rooster Cogburn, and hopefully, we'll see more of him in future books.... With the death of the incomparable Louis L'Amour, there is a need for somebody to fill the vacuum. One of the established writers who will claim his share of the range is undoubtedly R. C. House."

—Don Coldsmith, Spur Award–winning author of the *Spanish Bit Saga*

Lacey Bonner: A big, drunken brute of a man, he and Sam Cass had been fired for getting too familiar with Matt Antrim's wife, Stella—and Bonner wanted revenge. He only meant to beat Antrim to a pulp, but when the rancher cried out while Sammy was raping Stella, he silenced him with a bullet....

Sam Cass: After Lacey killed both Matt and Stella, Cass sobered up enough to realize that their greatest danger would come not from the law, but from the three remaining Antrim brothers. He was dead right....

"R. C. House is a writer of consummate skill, with both a deep love for and an intimate knowledge of the American West and its history. All these things come together in *Trackdown at Immigrant Lake*, a book that is destined for a place on everyone's Fifty Best list for generations to come."

—Loren Estleman, two-time Spur Award–winning author of *King of the Corner*

"In Cole Ryerson, marshal of Immigrant Lake, R. C. House has created a memorable Man of the Old West. House's work gets better with each book—*Sudden Gun* was terrific, *Trackdown at Immigrant Lake* is even better."

—Dale L. Walker, *Rocky Mountain News*,
president of the Western Writers of America

Cole Ryerson: As a young man, he'd learned everything he knew about tracking from Pat Graydon. He was glad to be on hand to ride with the old man, even if he'd rather be heading back to his home in New Mexico....

Pat Graydon: The aging sheriff could still walk as smoothly and silently as a snake. But he grew stiff in the saddle too easily now, and he was grateful to have Ryerson along on the trail of Bonner and Cass....

Kate Folsom: She was a beautiful, strong, and capable redhead, grown stronger through five years of privation on the Kansas prairie. Kate was tough enough to chase off Lacey Bonner and Sam Cass after they shot her man—and woman enough to make Cole Ryerson glad she'd insisted on coming with him....

"*Trackdown at Immigrant Lake* crackles with excitement. Cole Ryerson is a manhunter no one wants on his trail. From start to finish, this book draws a reader into the vortex of the action. R. C. House creates memorable characters and you'll be sorry to see them go when the last page is turned."

—Fred Bean, author of *The Last Warrior*

"R. C. House has crafted a vintage Western novel in *Trackdown at Immigrant Lake*. House captures that time after the Civil War when bold men ventured westward to seek their fortunes. In House's book, you can smell the burnt powder, taste the trail dust. He knows his guns; he knows the West. This is a superb entertainment, fast-moving, studded with characters plucked from our bloody past and kept alive on the printed page. One of the best traditional Westerns I've read lately."

—Jory Sherman, Spur Award–winning author of *The Medicine Horn*

Mitch Antrim: The oldest brother, and the meanest, he would not rest until he'd taken care of "family business" and avenged the death of Matt....

Mort Antrim: Ugly and vicious, he followed Mitch's lead in everything—including bullying Myles....

Myles Antrim: Mort's twin was feeble minded—but no less dangerous than his brothers. His fondest wish was to hang Cass and Bonner up by their heels and build a fire under their heads....

Praise for R. C. House's *The Sudden Gun*

"Without forsaking the shoot-'em-up tone of his title, House here offers a nicely drawn Portrait of the Outlaw as a Young Man.... House's careful, detailed narrative illuminates the emotional and physical torments that mold the Sanders brothers and shape their lives.... House's surprisingly affecting ending adds depth to a tale that transcends its genre."

—*Publishers Weekly*

Books by R. C. House

Ryerson's Manhunt*
Spindrift Ridge*
Requiem for a Rustler*
Warhawk
Trackdown at Immigrant Lake*
Drumm's War (*with Bill Bragg*)
The Sudden Gun
Vengeance Mountain
So the Loud Torrent

*Published by POCKET BOOKS

For orders other than by individual consumers, Pocket Books grants a discount on the purchase of **10 or more** copies of single titles for special markets or premium use. For further details, please write to the Vice-President of Special Markets, Pocket Books, 1230 Avenue of the Americas, New York, NY 10020.

For information on how individual consumers can place orders, please write to Mail Order Department, Paramount Publishing, 200 Old Tappan Road, Old Tappan, NJ 07675.

RYERSON'S MANHUNT

R.C. HOUSE

POCKET BOOKS
New York London Toronto Sydney Tokyo Singapore

The sale of this book without its cover is unauthorized. If you purchased this book without a cover, you should be aware that it was reported to the publisher as "unsold and destroyed." Neither the author nor the publisher has received payment for the sale of this "stripped book."

This book is a work of fiction. Names, characters, places and incidents either are products of the author's imagination or are used fictitiously. Any resemblance to actual events or locales or persons, living or dead, is entirely coincidental.

An *Original* Publication of POCKET BOOKS

POCKET BOOKS, a division of Simon & Schuster Inc.
1230 Avenue of the Americas, New York, NY 10020

Copyright © 1994 by R. C. House

All rights reserved, including the right to reproduce
this book or portions thereof in any form whatsoever.
For information address Pocket Books, 1230 Avenue
of the Americas, New York, NY 10020

ISBN: 0-671-87243-5

First Pocket Books printing April 1994

10 9 8 7 6 5 4 3 2 1

POCKET and colophon are registered trademarks of
Simon & Schuster Inc.

Cover art by Colin Backhouse

Printed in the U.S.A.

For Sallie
For your lifetime of faith in your kid brother.

✦ PROLOGUE ✦

COLORADO (AP)—

In 1993 road crews straightening a stretch of curving highway near the Wyoming-Colorado border unearthed a curious artifact of the old West. As they cleared away a dense and overgrown thicket of trees, brush, and vines that apparently no one had penetrated in nearly a century, a regularly shaped pile of rocks was discovered under the natural debris. Recognizing an early, crude burial site, they notified the authorities. The cairn was respectfully opened. Whatever or whoever the rocks cloaked had disintegrated over time. Only a few shirt and fly buttons were found, along with a simple belt buckle, some century-old coins, a badly rusted jackknife, and a gold tooth. Under a thick mat of dead twigs and leaf mold, they also uncovered a marble tombstone that had stood at the head of the rude crypt, but had fallen over. It had been professionally cut, polished, and inscribed:

SHERIFF PATRICK GRAYDON
1817–1876
Slain by an assassin's bullet
Placed by his friend
Cole Ryerson

Both the old towns of Medicine Springs and Patchknife some miles away—and their records—had long since themselves gone to dust. To this day the crypt and its contents remain a mystery.

1

In Stella Antrim's cringing terror, everything was fuzzy and indistinct. Out of the stark fright that had robbed her of any clarity in her thinking, she was only vaguely aware of the beating Matt was taking at the hands of Lacey Bonner and Sam Cass in the fenced-in corral.

"Hit the son of a bitch, Sam!" she heard Bonner shout, choking on his own exertion. She heard the dull thud of a fist connecting somewhere with flesh and bone, and heard her husband's muffled belch of pain.

Terror tore away all thoughts of the past or future. Stella Antrim's thinking was flaming red with a soul-rending fright. Her fear-dilated eyes refused to function, turning the barnyard puddles from last night's rain into dazzling suns of blinding light, while inside the stable where she had fled to cower against a pile of musty hay, pitch-darkness swam around her, with nothing familiar taking shape. As she looked toward the door to the barnyard, a glaring rectangle of blazing light, the haze of yellow midday sun diffused the door's frame in her befuddled vision.

Grunting with another blow to Matt Antrim's head, Sam Cass shouted, "What about the woman, Lacey?"

"She'll get hers directly. First we take this bastard to account."

An agonized bellow split the air around Stella Antrim's consciousness as big Lacey Bonner's sledgehammer fist again plowed into Matt's midsection. Stella drew herself smaller, into a quaking huddle against the hay.

Like a penned, tortured animal inside the corral, Matt tried to get away from his former hired hands, slipping and sliding in mud and manure made slick by the night's rain. Each time the pair caught him, each time a fist thudded with sickening impact and sound into Matt's body or head, Stella winced in shared agony.

Matt Antrim, splattered with slimy mud and filth and his own blood, at last splashed into the pools and puddles of the corral, incapable of rising or resisting. On hands and knees, head down and vomiting, Matt knelt like a whipped pup, totally beaten.

The drunken beast that was Lacey Bonner put a huge boot against the small of Antrim's back and shoved him down to squish inert into the barnyard slop.

"You jes' gonna leave him lay there, Lacey?"

"Hell, no, we ain't. Tie him to the gawdamn fence. None of this comin' to and sneakin' to the house for his scattergun while we're in havin' fun with the woman. Get that piece of rope hanging from the fence there, Sam."

Together they dragged the limp body to the corral rails and tied Matt, spread-eagle fashion, snubbing his outstretched arms to the top rail, his spread feet to the lower one. Antrim's head sagged and his tongue lolled in his unconsciousness.

"Now, Sammy," Bonner enthused, "let's go have us a look-see at that little Miss High-and-Mighty." Stella heard them sloshing through the mud toward the stable. Lacey Bonner's voice turned coy. "Stella? You in there, Stella?"

Bonner's massive frame blotted out the sunlight coming through the door, the silhouette of a giant. Stella dug her heels deeper into the hay, whimpering like a small child, her wide eyes centered in terror on the beast in the doorway. Sam Cass craned his neck to peer around Bonner into the murky depths of the stable.

Bonner leaned one muddy hand easily on the door frame. "Well, lookie here what we caught in our traps, Sammy. Laying there all ripe and ready for the pluckin'. Get our bottle out of my saddlebags."

"Why do I always—"

Bonner spun around and backhanded Cass in the head. Sam, only somewhat less huge than Bonner, reeled with the blow, drunkenly trying to keep his balance. "Go get the gawdamn jug!" Bonner commanded.

When Cass trudged back, Bonner rudely snatched the big blue bottle of amber fluid from his grip, tore out the cork with his teeth, spit it away and threw back his head for a long pull. Still holding the bottle, he rasped a sleeve across his dripping mouth. "There now," he said, "that hits the spot. Here." He handed the bottle to Cass and moved off toward the mound of haystack where Stella cowered. "Have you a stiff one, Sam. Now comes the good part. What we been waitin' for."

"Mr. Bonner, please," a voice from somewhere within her pleaded, sounding weak and timid. "Take anything you want. Just go and leave us alone."

"Oh, sure, missy. We gonna get what we want. And you got it!" Bonner strode toward her, his heavy boots resounding on the stable's mud floor, hammered hard as rock by hooves and boots.

Cass, holding the bottle, materialized out of the darkness beside Bonner. Terror threw a tight chain around Stella's throat. No words would come. With her arms, she tried to cover her head and body in protection, drawing herself up into a ball.

Bonner crouched over her, a rude hand stroking the calf of one leg. "Let's see what proper ladies wear under these long dresses, Sam."

As she shrunk back with no escape, Cass eased down beside her. His callused palm caressed her throat and slid down under her dress top to savor her fullness. "Oh, this is nice, Lacey," Cass cooed.

"You damn betcha. And Sam, because you was such a nice fella to go fetch the bottle, I'm gonna let you go first with her." Stella, powerless to resist, felt Bonner pull the full skirts of her dress up over her knees. "Why, look at that, would you, Sam. This is what a man'll find under here. Little white knee britches, all fluffy and nice."

Stella Antrim briefly found her voice. "Mr. Bonner, Mr. Cass ... please."

"Please to help you outta them frilly things, huh, honey?" Bonner reefed up the skirt's hemline and reached for the pantaloons' exposed pucker string at her waist. "Gawdamn," he grunted as the muslin garment resisted. Stella was lifted off the hay as Bonner continued to jerk at the waistband. It stretched and popped, ripping the cloth. Bonner eagerly continued to shred the material to get it away from her body.

Bonner cooed again. "Now there y'are, Sam. What d'ya think a that sight for sore eyes?"

"Nice, Lacey. Nice."

"Tell you what, Sam. I'm gonna go out and take my ease with the bottle and leave you children to your fun. She gets feisty, Sam, you jus' cuff her one, y'hear. She'll gentle."

Stella Antrim had lost all touch with reality. She was vaguely aware of Lacey Bonner pushing himself up heavily off the stable floor, away from her, and slouching toward the glaring doorway. In her terror for what was to come, she flinched to slide away from

Sam Cass, his face leering as he moved to get down over her. He grabbed her rudely by the neck to force her body back under his, choking off her breath as he muscled her into position. In the dim light, a trickle of drool glistened at the side of his mouth. The same hand that had yanked at her throat slid under the back of her head and he drew it toward his hungry, slobbery mouth. A groping hand forced her bare thigh sidewise. Stella's choked sob of resistance escaped as a hiss from Cass's unwanted, animal kiss.

Her frantic hands pushing at his chest yielded under his massive body. Her thrashing under him was meaningless once his suffocating weight crushed down on her as though she were a feather.

Outside, Lacey Bonner had paused in the sunlight to point the bottom of the bottle at the sky and curl his lips around the ample neck for a long pull. He wandered to where the body of Matt Antrim sagged like a man crucified against the bonds holding him to the corral rails.

Antrim groggily and slowly regained his senses. His eyelids fluttered, his head trying to come up against the exhaustion and pain that made it weigh a ton on his neck.

A woman's loud, high-pitched shriek split the silence in one long, frantic, piercing scream of pain and panic. The cry was cut short as the mouth forming it was slammed with a pile-driver fist.

Antrim came alert, his head snapping up. "Stella..." he started. Lacey Bonner arced a hand toward his hip, jerking free a long-barreled six-gun. With one swing he brought the gun up, plowed it into Antrim's midsection and sprung the trigger. "Shut up, gawdammit!" The muzzle blast was muffled in the thick muscle of Antrim's abdomen. Again his head sagged.

An hour later, two drunk but pleasantly fatigued former hands of the Matt Antrim Ranch swung up on their horses and prepared to ride away from the place whose owners they had so thoroughly ravaged. "What the hell'd you do to Antrim?" Sam Cass asked, lurching slightly as he hit the saddle.

"Shot the dinkpecker! He was tellin' me he didn't like the notion of you in there lollygaggin' with his squaw, Sam. So I give him what-for to shut him up and not disturb your fun." In mock formality he added, "What are friends for, Sammy?"

"Well, I'm a sunbeam! You ain't a half-bad sort after all, Lacey," Cass crowed, cackling.

"Bet you're so drunk, Sam, you couldn't put his eye out with your hogleg from here."

"Well, jus' you don't—" Cass said, unleashing his six-gun and letting a round fly at the dead man hanging from the corral fence. Antrim's head jerked with the impact and dropped back to loll on its neck.

"Whee-oo!" Bonner cheered. "Done it, 'y God! Damn good shootin'!"

Bonner fired again at the body, seeing blood and cloth and flesh and crusted mud scatter as the corpse was torn by another bullet.

A disheveled Stella Antrim sagged against the stable's door frame, her long and full skirt torn to expose ripped and bloody muslin pantaloons clumsily drooping between her knees and ankles.

"Matt!" she screamed, seeing her dead husband draped on the fence. "For God's sake! Matt!"

"Aw, hell!" Bonner growled. He swung the gun, still in his hand, and fired at the hysterical woman.

Stella Antrim's body was slammed back inside the stable. Only her feet, in high-heeled button shoes, projected out the doorway. The feet trembled and jerked as life ebbed out of her battered, ravaged body.

"Come on, Sam," Bonner said, growing a bit lucid from the blood they'd spilled. "We gotta make tracks. The law won't rest easy till they see our necks stretched for this. We won't be able to hide till we're safe at home in Texas."

Sam Cass's eyes now went wide as the enormity of what they had done dawned on him. "Hell, Lacey, it ain't the law that scares me. I don't take to the notion of them Antrim boys comin' after us."

"Yeah," Bonner intoned soberly. "We better git outta here!"

2

The day was too beautiful for a manhunt.

The two lawmen had been out of sight of Patchknife for more than an hour in the rolling country marked by grasslands and occasional gray rock outcroppings as the land gently rolled away from them or sloped up gradually. It was, Cole Ryerson thought, easy country to ride in.

Washed and still crisp from the rain of two nights before, the land this morning gleamed like a fresh-scrubbed baby. The sky held a depth of blue equal to that of a beautiful woman's eyes. Its great turquoise bowl over them was framed all around the two riders with massive billows of rich cumulus fluff piled in great mountainous gobs.

The air, too, was washed to a new purity, cleansing Ryerson's mind even of the stench of what he knew of the mindless and brutal double murder of Patchknife rancher Matt Antrim and his wife Stella. Under him, his horse's hooves crunched in grass lush from its recent drink of pure rain.

Beside Ryerson, the normally open, friendly face of the Patchknife sheriff, Pat Graydon, was clamped tight with the urgency of the manhunt. Graydon's concern was compounded by the knowledge that the dead man's three brothers would also be out here somewhere searching for the two murderers, Sam Cass and Lacey Bonner.

Ryerson studied Graydon, a big man, big-boned with large features. His strength of character showed in the craggy weathered lines of his face. His heavy, masculine nose was matched by large ears with pendulous lobes. Graydon's full, steel-gray hair, under a good-quality Stetson fit straight to his head, curled and looped around the ears. Pat Graydon was a man most everyone liked instantly, but he could also make enemies.

Graydon spoke as though it was a thought out loud. "If the Antrim boys get to them first, there won't be much left over even for the buzzards." His eyes were not on the trail, but far away, as though he was looking at the distant mountains that wore the thick clouds as crowns on their peaks. Despite the clouds, the land around Ryerson and Graydon was drenched in sunlight.

It was magnificent country, Ryerson thought. He wondered if the sky was larger here or in New Mexico, where he had come from and was heading back to when his old friend, Graydon, appealed for his help.

Graydon was getting too old for this sort of demand on his spirit and his stamina, Ryerson thought, still studying the aging lawman. Old times—the good times and the troubled times—insisted that Ryerson stay to do what he could to help, even though he was a stranger to this land, with no real vested interest in Graydon's quest.

They had pledged their friendship and support years before, when Graydon had finally left the harsh life of an Army scout in the New Mexico Territory. And, Ryerson knew, promises made were debts unpaid. Graydon had saved Federal Marshal Cole Ryerson's chestnuts a few times in their years together. Now it was Ryerson's turn.

"How can you be so sure those two did it, Pat?"

"Oh, I'm purely persuaded they're the ones we're after all right. The finger points in no other direction."

Ryerson, on his way home after taking two military prisoners up the Santa Fe Trail to Fort Leavenworth, had passed near the Patchknife Basin and rode by to say howdy to an old friend, only to find him knee deep in trouble. Though Ryerson was much younger than Graydon, the pair of them had worked together in scouting for the Army or in bringing scalawags to justice down near the border in New Mexico. Graydon, who'd taught Ryerson much of what he knew, had retired from Army scouting duty, and taken the law-keeping job in Patchknife for his old age.

Ryerson had built on what he'd learned from the seasoned Graydon, and had gone on as a federal marshal to become one of the top trackers and lawmen in the Southwest. Now he put the same savvy to work in Graydon's high plains country.

One thing was certain, he thought, as they rode the sprawl of a handsome land: this situation was a tight one for old Pat. Two mad-dog killers had to be brought to justice, and the three Antrim brothers were coming up behind them to take matters into their own hands, the law be damned.

"It's my very good fortune that this should come up while you were in town, Cole," Graydon said, interrupting Ryerson's reverie. "If I had thought of the one man I would want along with me on this, it would have been you. Divine providence, that's what it is. Divine providence! You can't know how relieved I am that you arranged things to ride with me."

"You gave it to me pretty fast back in Patchknife last night, Pat. But I caught enough to know that you had your hands full, old pard. If you were on my home ground and I were in such a jam, I know you'd be the first one to step up and offer to help."

"When you put it that way, you purt near said it all."

Ryerson took another deep breath of the clear, crisp air, feeling its clarity sting his nostrils and its strength flood his body, leaving him a-tingle. He damned the grisly mission that kept him from riding happily toward New Mexico this very morning. The brutal nature of the murders—about which he had only scant details—could throw a dark cloud over the most glorious of days, as this one was, particularly for a man involved in the chase after the suspects.

Again Graydon interrupted Ryerson's thoughts. "It's pretty clear," he said. "Old Antrim—well, he wasn't that old—hired these two last spring when hands were hard to come by. Got stuck with a couple of doozies, if you ask me. Day before yesterday, it seems, Matt Antrim came home to find the pair of them being a little forward with Stella—Mrs. Antrim. Oh, she was a proper woman, no question. But Cass and Bonner were getting a bit pushy. There and then, Matt gave them their wages and told them to roll up their gear and ride on."

"Hardly grounds for suspecting them, Pat," Ryerson said.

"Under the circumstances, it'd hardly be enough. But there's more. They were riled. They'd tried to sign on with a couple of other outfits here in the basin, and the bosses saw through them. Figured this pair was trouble about to brew. This was before Antrim put them on. After he cashiered them, they came on into town that afternoon and spent most of their wages tying one on."

Graydon reined up to give his horse a rest. He squirmed around to ease his position in the saddle and scan the miles of open country stretching away in all directions. Below them, though there didn't seem to be any water in it, was a great cleft in the land, which in New Mexico might be called a draw. Around here, Ryerson knew, it was known as a coulee. Graydon's eyes probed the awesome distance through air almost clear enough to see forever.

"I have a hunch we ought to keep pushing south," he said.

"This is your land, Pat, your people. You know best."

Graydon, twisted in the saddle to ease his butt cramps, settled back into it with a low groan. Ryerson, resting a few feet behind, shook his head. In their days of scouting just north of the line, he'd known Pat Graydon to be in the saddle from morning star to moonrise and never so much as stop to take a leak.

"As these kind usually are," Graydon called back as Ryerson spurred his horse up beside him, "they got mouthy in town in the bar over at the Patchknife House and spilled everything that had happened. They claimed Stella flirted with them for months and was only waiting for Matt to be gone long enough so each of them could have a turn. They left town before noon roaring drunk, and had already allowed that before they left this neck of the woods, they were going to go back and clean old Antrim's plow and give Stella something they figured she'd been looking for."

"Now it makes sense to bring them in for questioning, Pat."

Graydon wasn't through. "In the afternoon, Joe Sherman rode by that way and found Matt and Stella. I was called out. It wasn't pretty. The two of them had been worked over mighty rough before they were killed. Beat Matt to a pulp, and each of them probably took Stella down in the barn. They'd roped Matt to the corral fence and popped a few rounds into him as they rode out. Killed the woman in the barn."

"Vicious. Ugly," Ryerson said. "We're likely to have our hands full."

"In more ways than one. I still don't see how they

got the drop on Matt Antrim. He was tough, tough as they come, with a mean streak in him, too. I don't imagine the thing with his wife the other day was the first time he'd had words with the pair of them. They could've been nursing some pretty old hurts. A man can get dug that way, y'know, even if he ain't got a mean streak. Let it build up, and when it comes to a head, it's Katie bar the door."

"Assuming Cass and Bonner did it, you seem intent on moving south after them, Pat."

"Stands to reason again, Cole. You know damned well yourself in this business that you could pick any point on the compass, and unless you know exactly where a desperado is going to hole up, you could be going in the wrong direction. Patchknife is due north. They'll not likely turn back that way. East of Matt's place, but not far, is the old Antrim homestead. The old folks are gone, but Matt's three brothers still work the place. None of them has taken a woman, and if you knew them, you'd understand why. All you have to do is look west and see why Cass and Bonner wouldn't go that way. The mountains. Cowboys have little use for mountains, regardless how good they are to hide in. These're grassland men, high plains men."

"So far you make sense, Pat."

"Most of the drifters through here are Texans. Come up this far with a cattle drive and maybe it gets wiped out or maybe they're misfits who get to mixing it up with some of the other hands on the trail and get cashiered." Graydon seemed to stop in mid-thought; he looked anxiously back over his shoulder.

"I figured the Antrims will get on the trail this morning," Pat continued. "I don't exactly look forward to seeing them out here. Well, like I say, maybe these bozos were headed back home after a trail drive and blew their roll in a poker game or soppin' up booze or chasin' women. So, they took a job for a few months, maybe, with one of the local outfits—like Antrim. It sticks in my mind that Cass and Bonner were out of Texas. Just about everything below here ends up in Texas anyway. So I figure them to head south."

"Got any particular trail or route in mind?"

"About the only one they'd take, I suppose. You'll see, Cole. They'll be flowing along the line of least resistance, and that's good enough for me. They're probably not bright enough to move into strange territory to cover their tracks. The land keeps dropping through here, generally. To the east it's chopped up and broken with box canyons and coulees and badlands. Generally rough going. West, the land gentles some but gets rough again as it rises toward the hills. Naw, Cole, we'll cut their sign before night, or first thing in the morning, I'm betting. With any kind of luck, by tomorrow forenoon we'll be headed home with Sam Cass and Lacey Bonner in our string."

"Sounds like you got it all packaged and tied with a neat little ribbon, Pat," Ryerson said cheerily.

"Wish I did." Graydon sounded glum.

"Meaning?"

"The fly in the ointment. The Antrim boys. Oh, it shouldn't be any trick for a savvy scout and lawman to get the drop on them. They're bullies, clumsy ones at that. Don't know straight up about gunfighting. Hell, son, you and I corraled Little Pete and his Apaches down north of the line. Compared to that, this'll be like roping a newborn calf. It's the trip back that's got me on edge. We'll be riding right into the teeth of three damned mad Antrim boys who'll want to see Cass and Bonner dead, and the hell with justice. They're bound to be out here somewhere. I know them. No patience with due process of law and the hangman. If we get in their way, or keep them from having their way, we'll be as much fair game to them as Bonner and Cass."

"The fly in the ointment for sure," Ryerson said.

"Four of them. Originally. Matt was the youngest,

and judged against his brothers, was a lamb. But Matt could be mean. Plumb mean. Mitchell, they call him Mitch—rhymes with a son of something or other, and it fits—is the oldest and pretty much runs things. Then there's the twins, Morton, known as Mort, and Myles. Why their father gave them all names starting with M is beyond me, but that's it."

"Huh!" Ryerson snorted. "Rough bunch, eh?"

"Like a frozen cob on a cold morning. Mort was the firstborn of the twins, and they say he took his sweet old time being hatched. Myles had to wait, and I guess it affected his head some way. They say all that had a lot to do with Myles winding up a little short on his tally, if you know what I mean."

"Feebleminded?"

Graydon nodded as he led them down slopes of golden, winter-cured grass. Beyond the coulee, Ryerson could see that the land opened up again; a broad, flat plain shimmered in distant sunlight. By all indications, as they rode down the head of the broad, gentle cleft in the land, the country was less rolling down there in the direction they traveled.

"A mite short on his tally," Graydon said again. "Backward, as decent folks say. But I daresay Myles can kill as good as Mort or Mitch. His brothers don't have a corner on meanness in the family. Just that Myles is more unpredictable."

Ryerson's keen eyes were attracted to movement on the slow, rolling bench over the draw they moved down. Atop the grassy east rim and silhouetted against the morning sky, three riders had come up and stopped, watching as the lawmen rode down the coulee. Ryerson's instincts perked. Something sinister marked the riders on the knoll.

"Pat! Up there on the ridge. To our left."

Graydon's eyes came up to spot the trio, and Ryerson saw his face tense.

"Would that be the Antrims?" Ryerson asked.

"Sure as hell."

3

"What do we do, Pat? Ignore them?"

"I wish it were that easy. Their brother and his wife are dead, and they're out for blood."

The three on the hill stood their horses, watching the two, a half mile away in the coulee, with an air of evil evident even at that distance. Ryerson was familiar with their posture in the saddle. Hostile Indians paused to study white intruders the same way—often just before they rode to the attack.

"The longer we sit here," Graydon said, "the more they'll think we're plotting against them. They're that kind. They're sure the only reason we're out here is to rob them of their sweet revenge."

"Do we ride up that way and talk with them?"

"Might help. It's all we can do at this point. I might suggest to them that if they get in our way, they'll be obstructing justice."

"From what you tell me, that's the least of their worries."

"It's all we've got."

"Looks like we meet them halfway. Here they come."

Graydon and Ryerson wheeled their horses and

started up toward the grassy knoll. Despite the glories of the sunlit land, the air around them had turned tight and tense, as before a storm.

"Should we be ready for action?" Ryerson asked softly. "Is there likely to be gunplay?"

"A man ought to be ready for anything, I suppose, from characters of this type. Ahh, it's doubtful. Hot words, maybe. Depends on how it goes. Stay alert."

Riding up to the Antrims as they came down, Ryerson looked them over, taking their measure in case drastic action was called for. It was the best way, as Pat Graydon had said. The Antrims rode through tall grass toyed with by a fresh breeze. It stirred the grass around the horses' hoofs and snapped at the riders' clothing and hair and hat brims. It did little to detract from the ominous feel of the moment.

They were dark and mean, but capable-looking men, accustomed to getting what they set out for even if it meant bulling their way through by brute force. These kind, Ryerson knew, were fairly easy to buffalo. It was the smooth, slick, and glib ones that offered too many imponderables.

The man in the lead would be Mitch Antrim, Ryerson thought, with the twins, Mort and Myles, riding side by side somewhat behind Mitch and to his right. While the three bore a family resemblance, the twins had identical builds, coloring, and facial structure.

A blank expression and a sagging chin and open mouth set Myles apart from Mort, and he rode his horse with less command than his twin. As they neared the Antrims, Ryerson could see that Myles had a habit of running his tongue out over his open lips, and the sidewise set of his head suggested a man not in full control of his faculties.

By contrast, Mort Antrim's features were tightly set but alert, with the narrowed eyelids of a man adept at brutality. Their horses showed poor care and appeared to have been hazed a great deal. A touch of irony came into Ryerson's thinking that these men could be as ugly and vicious as the pair he and Graydon were tracking.

"Graydon!" Mitch called as they came close enough for hailing. "You and your friend there can go back to town now. We'll take it from here." Harsh determination clanged in Mitch's words.

"I believe we need to talk this over, Mitch," Graydon called, riding closer. Ryerson allowed Pat the lead, holding back as Mitch and Graydon brought their horses close enough to palaver. The Antrim twins eased their gaits, stretching the distance between them and Mitch. Ryerson sensed that the possibility of gunplay was very real.

Ryerson was aware of being looked over himself, by Mort Antrim, no doubt wondering about him, taking his measure against the time that the two of them might clash. Myles Antrim's eyes, meanwhile, appeared to fix on nothing; again his tongue went around in its course of licking his lips.

"Mitch, I sympathize with you in your loss of Matt," Graydon said.

"Evil deeds by evil men," Antrim said flatly.

Graydon stared at Mitch, surprised by such philosophy from the big rancher. "Granted. And we're on our way to bring in Cass and Bonner for questioning in the deaths of your brother and his wife."

"They done it sure enough. You don't have to go mealy-mouthin' around askin' 'em did they do it, Graydon. There ain't no questions needin' to be asked. Them two need stringin' up."

"Due process of law, Mitch. Marshal Ryerson and I will return them for trial."

"Ryerson? Is that the outlander with you?"

"Marshal Cole Ryerson has a federal appointment with Judge Isaac Winfield's court at Fort Walker, New Mexico. He'd stopped by my place on his way back there when all this came up. I asked him along. I'll need his help. You may have heard of him as 'Boot Hill Cole.' "

Mitch dismissed Ryerson's background with a grunt. "Well, you can send him packin', and you can go on back and hole up in Patchknife, Graydon. We'll take it from here. This is Antrim business that needs 'tendin' to. By us. A family matter."

Graydon paused, as if hunting in his head for the right words. "Mitch, I'm sorry. I know how you feel. But I'm the law in Patchknife, and the law has been broken in my jurisdiction. Marshal Ryerson and I will bring them in, you can be sure of that."

Mitch Antrim looked past Graydon at Ryerson. "Hey, you there, Boot Lick Man. You better talk some sense into this old coot. Get it th'ough his head we don't want no one standin' in our way! Law or no law!"

Ryerson bristled at the slurs against him and Graydon. Looking at Mitch Antrim, he suddenly felt he had all sorts of reasons for being in on this manhunt.

Myles Antrim edged his horse closer. "We ... we gonna hang 'em upside down an' built a fa'r under they heads," he said eagerly. It was the first time he had spoken; Ryerson heard a voice that was high-pitched and childish.

Ryerson ignored the imbecile. "You ought to listen to reason, Mr. Antrim," he said to Mitch. "Sheriff Graydon and I will bring in the suspects."

Mitch glared at Ryerson. "Suspects!? You only suspect them two? Well, you two 'lawmen' sure as hell got cowshit packed in your ears. I told you they done it, plain as the nose on your face. Now let me and my brothers by and we'll get out there and save the law a lot of time and trouble, not to mention taxpayers' money. Make it easy on yourself. There's things you should be attending to in Patchknife, Graydon. You're gettin' too old for this kind of thrashin' around anyways."

"Don't do it, Mitch," Graydon warned. "Don't continue on this insane course, or you'll wind up as guilty as Cass and Bonner."

"Oh, you own up now that they're guilty?"

"No question in my mind. But I'm not the one to decide. That'll be up to a jury to weigh the evidence against them."

"Aw, horseshit! Get on back to town like I told you, Graydon. We're ridin' after that pair, and we'll kill anybody that gets in our way. Right, Mort?"

Ryerson felt his right arm and wrist tense; his hand was mere inches from the wear-polished wood grips of his holstered cap-and-ball Colt Navy. Mort Antrim said nothing, but his sinister eyes slid from Graydon to Ryerson and back, glinting with his assent.

"There's just you," Mitch said, his voice rising. "A broke-down old has-been, Graydon, and some mealy-mouthed outlander. And I don't particularly cotton to outlanders mixin' in Antrim business. It's you two against me and my brothers."

Graydon's voice was flat, but carried a razor's edge.

"Mitch, ride on if you will, but don't you or any of your brothers get in our way. If you do, so help me, the name Antrim will disappear from Patchknife Basin. There's one down and only three left to go."

"Well, goddamn you! Is that a threat, Graydon?"

"A warning or a threat. Take it any way you want."

Mitch started for his gun, but was stopped by a warning shout from Ryerson, who had edged his horse closer to the pair. The muzzle of Ryerson's .36 Navy, small though it was, had the appearance of a mountain howitzer in Mitch Antrim's eyes as his fingertips began a nervous dance against the checkered grips of his still-holstered six-gun. With Antrim's first menacing gesture toward his gun, Ryerson had unlimbered the Navy that fast. Antrim pulled in his horns.

"You're pretty quick with that, Mr. Boot Hill Man," he said, his face carrying what passed for a sheepish grin. Still, Ryerson knew, Mitch hadn't budged an inch from his position.

"I learned from a good man. That one right there," Ryerson responded.

Graydon's right hand rested casually along the bulk of his tied-down six-gun holster. It jutted alongside his wrist in a businesslike way. The movement of his hand a mere inch or so would unleash it and the fury of a slug backed by forty grains of powder. At this range it would kick a man the size of Mitch Antrim clear out of the saddle.

Graydon frowned, tipping his head down so his tight-clenched eyes glared at Mitch from under his hat brim.

"My advice to you, Antrim, is to take your brothers and ride back to your place. Wait there till Ryerson and I bring in Bonner and Cass. I'll make sure you're invited to testify against them."

Myles Antrim's voice intruded, his voice whiny and childish. "Mitch, you ... you mean we don't git to hang 'em up by they heels and built a fa'r under they heads?"

"Shut up, Myles!" Mitch roared. "Mort, make sure that brother of yours keeps still. Judas!"

Mort Antrim whipped off his hat and angrily whacked Myles on the shoulder. "Shut up!" he yelled. Myles's eager face fell and he cowered in the saddle. Ryerson heard a soft whimper as the half-wit swung his horse around and pulled back a ways to watch the goings-on like a schoolboy rejected from a playground game.

"Well, Graydon," Mitch said. "You and your boy won this one. Next time it'll be different." He took a long moment to glare at Graydon, who had said no more but matched Mitch Antrim stare for stare. When he was done scowling at Graydon, Mitch swung his intent glare at Ryerson.

"Watch your step in these parts, New Mexico lawman. Watch it close every step of the way. We ain't no blanket Injuns you're dealin' with around here."

Bulldozed for the moment, but defiant, making sure his movements weren't misunderstood, Mitch lifted the reins to bring his horse's head around and started at a slow walk back up the hill. Mort was right behind him. Myles sat his horse for a minute, watching them leave, seeming confused. Then he bounced in the saddle, kneed his horse's ribs and started after his brothers, but kept a respectable distance, as though he sensed some punishment was in store.

Ryerson watched them go up the hill, headed for the knoll where he'd first seen them. "Think they'll stay out of it, Pat?"

"Oh, hell, they'll stay in it right to the end. What I don't know is how we'll handle it. I do know that now we'll have to keep our rear and our flank protected while we probe ahead for the two hardcases we're really after. You'll have to be the eyes in back of my head, Cole."

"We've worked that way a few times before, pard," Ryerson said. "You think he meant business when he started for his gun?"

"Mitch Antrim's not cagey enough to bluff. Glad you stopped him. I don't think Mitch figures he has much to lose at this point. He knows if they lynch Cass and Bonner—and they have every intention of doing just that—the law will be after them for murder. We're the law. With us out of the way, he's got a clear trail."

"Killing us won't hang him any higher."

"You got a direct way of putting things, you know that, Cole? Let's get moving. The longer we sit, the farther Cass and Bonner are from us."

Together they urged their mounts down the hillside to the bottom of the coulee where they had first spotted the Antrims. Down there, Ryerson looked back to see the three as they had been—watching as the lawmen moved away toward the wide mouth of the broad ravine.

"They're out for blood, Pat. That Myles *is* the scary one. He'll delight in torture. It's going to be tight, finding Bonner and Cass and getting them—and ourselves—back to Patchknife in one piece."

"You damn betcha." Graydon's big paws, with stubby but capable fingers, the backs wrinkled and knobby with age and weathering, fidgeted a bit with the reins as Ryerson watched. "Does this one scare you some, Pat?"

"You're the only one that'll know." Graydon looked up and to his right. "Sun's a bit past noon and we're headed due south. You game for lunch in the saddle with some jerky?"

"Buffalo?"

"The best. Killed and smoked and seasoned it myself."

"Sounds good. I'm game," Ryerson said.

"About four hours of steady riding should put us in some pretty campin' country. Rough, but good. We might find we're sharin' bedding ground with Cass and Bonner. I don't know. It would suit me fine the fewer night camps we have to make with those two when we head back. Country's generally open. By day we'll be able to ride free of the Antrims. What happens after dark is anybody's guess."

"Let's hope we find them tonight."

As they worked their way out of the sloping and wide end of the coulee and into the broad plain below, Ryerson glanced back the way they had come to where they'd left the Antrims perched on the rim watching them go.

"Pat," he said, "here they come. Back there. About two miles."

Graydon didn't look. "It figures." He pursed his lips and shook his head in resignation.

"Well," Ryerson said. "We've already had our confrontation with them. Not much we can do now but keep going."

"Nope," Graydon said. "It's a free country."

4

"I haven't sighted them in more than an hour," Ryerson said, with the sun starting its trek down into the mountains to the west. The broad grassland they had ridden into at noon finally gave way after several hours to chopped-up country with streams chewing their way past craggy obstacles of tumbled boulders for them to ride over or around. Trees, mostly aspen and cottonwoods, grew thickly here with no rhyme or reason, with scrub growth for the riders to veer around and slow down their pace.

Graydon's words carried an edge of anger, a touch of anxiety. "Hell, they're back there, don't worry about that." He urged his horse down a cutbank toward a nameless and shallow meandering stream.

For all Ryerson knew, they were lost in this stuff. This wasn't the kind of country he was used to moving through. Yet when the waning afternoon sun threw a dazzling sparkle at him through the thick leaves of a cottonwood, he looked at it directly over his right shoulder, proof that Graydon led them on a true southbound course.

"All we'd have to do would be to pull up one of these hills and sit quiet for half an hour or so, and you'd find out. They're on our trail keen as a pack of coonhounds."

"Oh, I believe you." Ryerson worked the reins to ride up the other side of the bank, his horse's nose almost against the rump of Graydon's animal. "This country is tough, but from what you tell me, I have the Antrims pegged as tougher."

"And more determined," Graydon said. "It's clear now what they're up to. They're going to let us find Cass and Bonner for them, and then move in and try to take them away from us. Or at least that's their intention. We'll be at the disadvantage with two prisoners to worry about, plus trying to save our own hides. They got their claws into us where the sun don't often shine, son."

"Like I keep telling you, Pat, I don't know this country. Is there nothing we can do?"

"You figure it. We've been in tight spots before." Graydon's words were grunted over his fatigue. Ryerson had known for hours that the old lawman was getting tired. They'd been on the trail since sunup, and the tension brought on by the showdown with the Antrims and being followed by them wasn't adding to Pat Graydon's peace of mind.

Again Ryerson was glad he was on hand to help his old friend. Graydon was one to fight and not give an inch until the bitter end. Without some kind of support, this clearly would be Pat Graydon's last stand.

"Nothing as tight as this one," Ryerson said.

"They're all different. Tell me what you think, Cole. Surely your experience tells you something."

"Okay. There's the obvious. The Antrims expect us to run the killers to ground and head them back to Patchknife, right?"

"Is there any other way, Cole?"

"Like you keep telling me, Pat, it's a big country. There are any number of points on the compass. Go back a way they don't expect. What are the options on the return leg?"

"We ride smack dab between some mighty big obstacles. To the west are the mountains. Tough, by God, going up in there. Some of it you can hardly make with a horse, much less with a couple of muley prisoners—and they will be. Taking them back will make the ride down here seem like a Sunday school picnic."

"What's the country like to the east?"

"What we used to call *malpais*. Rough, cut-up badlands. Box canyons, steep-sided everywhere. Even if we could make it through that stuff, there's a million places to get trapped. Then you either make a stand of it or ride right back into their guns."

"So what's left?"

"South, but that's no good. Nothing. No towns for a hundred miles. Tom Moon Dog's stage stop is about all I know of. Damned little water and not much game. And the jail and justice are the other way. We might take them to Moon Dog's and back home by stage, but that, too, is a long way around."

"Tom Moon Dog? Sounds like an Indian."

"One of your Apaches. He's close-mouthed about it; got a stiff knee from a cavalry bullet in one of those fights down there five or six years back. It gentled him. Decent enough man, but bitter; damn he's bitter! Pulls back like he's been bit if the subject comes up. Tolerates me well enough, but I feel he's got a hate for white-man authority, especially military. And I sometimes think one man in particular. But try to get more out of him and he closes up like a clam. He can take the hot, dry country out there—and the loneliness—so the stage line put him on at the way station. Keeps a small remuda of harness horses for fresh stage teams, and keeps food and provides a rest stop for passengers going through. He's south by west of here."

"Does the stage line go into Patchknife?"

"Way out of our way. Goes west of the mountains through a pass to Medicine Springs and over a northerly pass to Patchknife. Takes a couple of extra days that way."

"Good to know. Lose a horse, and a man might have to avail himself of the service."

"I don't know what we're fretting about. We haven't seen hide nor hair of Cass and Bonner. We don't even know if we've got prisoners for the Antrims to fight us over."

"No, but look there. Sure looks like an old camp to me."

The stream they followed wove its way through this wilderness like the coils of a snake, almost doubling back on itself at times. To their left, huge boulders rolling down from nearby hills in high water protected a broad circle of deep sand and gravel. A step or two away, the stream gurgled its difficult way south. Trees crowding the stream bank offered cover for the place and plenty of downed firewood; ideal for a night's stopover.

"Let's have a look-see," Ryerson said, walking his horse to the spot and getting down. In the center of a broad but irregular circle of sand, a pit had been dug for a warm fire that would be almost invisible, particularly after sticks and logs burned down. A mound of powdery gray ash filled it.

Graydon got down and tied his horse to a nearby tree before stiffly striding to where Ryerson looked over the spot. Ryerson crouched and rammed his hands deep into the ashes. "Still warm. See how the gravel's packed. Two men slept here last night. From the sign, they were big men."

Graydon stumped around the perimeter of huge gray boulders, peering, poking and rummaging for more sign. "Here," he called, stepping deep into the bushes. "Here's something." He came back to Ryerson, still at the fire pit, carrying an empty bottle. He held it out to Ryerson. A scant crescent of amber whiskey had drained into the bottom of it after the last drink and the bottle was tossed aside. The bottle was large, quart-size, Ryerson figured, and was thick, blue glass, wavy with imperfections.

"This came out of the Patchknife House or I'll eat your saddle," Graydon said. "And Sam Cass and Lacey Bonner emptied it."

"They picked a good spot," Ryerson said. "That puts them the better part of a day ahead of us, Pat. The sun's telling me we'll have to find us a spot to hole up for the night before long. I haven't seen a better spot than this one in a while. What do you think?"

"It's early enough. We might have visitors."

"If they think we're riding till dark, we may," Ryerson said.

"Oh, Mitch is savvy enough, Cole. Lived in and hunted this country all his life. A man develops a sixth sense after a while, if he's survived that long. I'll bet he's guessing that we'll settle in for the night pretty soon. He's probably picking his own hole for the three of them about now."

A soft breeze had come up, announcing the approach of evening. Leaves flickered in response. The soft sound of a gunshot, muffled by the distance, drifted down on a small gust from the north.

They stood quiet and listened. There were no more shots. Graydon walked to the center of the open area, his bedroll under his arm, and began untying and rolling out his blankets and soogans. "Well, sounds like the Antrims will have fresh meat tonight. I judge that round at a good mile and a half away."

"I'd say so," Ryerson said. "The air is different here than back where I come from, but my ears still agree with you."

"I have an idea," Graydon said as they busied themselves with making a camp. They had decided that the Antrims would do nothing more than follow them while Bonner and Cass were still at large. They planned to make a comfortable camp here, Antrims be damned. With the night's chill coming down close to the stream, despite another hour or so of light to see by, Ryerson started a small fire. It quickly radiated heat back to them off the boulders.

"Your idea?" Ryerson asked.

"We're in a full-moon phase. Those clouds this morning have thinned. Never did get cloudy directly over us. I say we sleep a few hours, until some after midnight. I wouldn't trust it trying to ride in this stuff. But the moon'll give us enough light to see to lead the horses. Five hours of good walking will put us that much closer to Cass and Bonner and that much farther from the Antrims. Maybe far enough to shake them."

"Depends on the menu," Ryerson said. Graydon looked at him, and seeing Ryerson's grin, shared it.

"Meaning?"

"I don't suppose we dare go out and hunt down some fresh meat the way they did."

"Wouldn't show much savvy. They'd have our location pinpointed, and head directly here in the morning. As it is, they may have a bit of hunting to get on our trail come dawn. This stuff we're in is damned thick. We chanced on this place, you know."

"So? The menu?"

"We march on short rations, son. Sowbelly and beans."

Ryerson groaned. "I should have known. And jerky for breakfast, I suppose." He didn't phrase it as a question.

"And jerky for breakfast," Graydon assured him.

They put a large can of beans to warm at the fire's edge. The salt pork sizzled in Graydon's little cast-iron spider. While waiting for their food to warm, they stretched out on their blankets, heads propped on saddles.

They were silent a long while, each with his own thoughts, Ryerson watching the slow approach of night. In this country, it seemed, dusk was a two-hour affair. The sun had long since gone to rest, turning everything gray. Still, it was possible to see quite a bit of their surroundings. Ryerson lay back, trying to relax despite his tension, and watched the sky going a deep gray through the leaves that meshed over his head and did a fair job of blocking out his view. His thoughts were interrupted by a hiss from Graydon. "Hark!"

They lay still, ears and senses tuned. Ryerson's right hand stroked the slick leather sheathing his Colt Navy. His Winchester was still in his saddle scabbard on the horse. The crackling in the brush from upstream drew closer and louder. Graydon rolled silently, drawing his revolver, and slid to the cover of a boulder. On his side of the fire, Ryerson did the same, finding a thick tree close at hand for cover.

Ryerson breathed lightly, not wanting the sounds from his nose and throat to rob his ears of significant sound. The crashing neared them.

Myles Antrim broke through the trees and walked past the circle of boulders, his attention focused on where he put his feet. He carried a short-barreled double shotgun as though he was hunting.

"Hello, Myles!" Graydon called cheerily, stepping away from the boulder, smiling. Myles jumped in surprise, but kept the shotgun in the crook of his arm. His head slowly pivoted in a sweep that took in the campsite and Graydon and Ryerson on either side of it. Myles's expression was blank and without emotion. His tongue started its course around his lips. When he'd finished, he spoke, haltingly.

"Ya—You're Sheriff Graydon, ain't ya?"

"That's right, Myles."

"We ... we gonna take them men away from you. They ... they kilt Matth—Matthew an' Stella. Mitch an' Mort an' me, we gonna ma—make you give them men to us. We gonna kill you, too, maybe." Myles's eyes glistened as he relished the thought.

"Do you want them to do that, Myles?" Graydon asked.

"Mitch an' Mort gonna hang 'em up by they ... by they heels, an' I—I git to built a fa'r under they heads." A broad grin of anticipation spread across his face.

"You'd better git now, Myles," Graydon said. "Be a good boy and go back to your camp with Mitch and Mort. We wouldn't want them to find you down there and slap you around, now would we?"

A cloud of concern came into his blank expression, and his tongue came out to lick the corners of his mouth.

"I—I gotta git back or Mort an' Mitch'll slap me around." Myles spun abruptly in an almost military about-face and headed back the way he had come.

"We . . ." he called as he disappeared into the brush. "We gonna kill you and take them men away from you ... an' hang 'em up, an' I git to built a fa'r under they heads." His voice trailed off into the distance.

Ryerson didn't speak until Myles's crashing through the brush quieted. "You said we start walking an hour after midnight, Pat?"

"That doesn't suit you?"

"Let's make it as soon as it's moon-bright."

"Put as many miles as we can between us and them as soon as possible?" Pat asked.

Ryerson's eyes acknowledged it.

5

Ryerson and Graydon had finished their simple meal of salt pork and beans washed down with strong coffee. Ryerson squatted comfortably on his heels near the fire, content with a full belly, regardless of the food's quality, cradling his coffee cup in his hands. Graydon perched on his saddle, almost out of the firelight in the growing dark.

In his square-set Stetson, with strong but open features in a big beefy face set on a solid neck, the big lawman looked at home and comfortable against the backdrop of trees and boulders, the flickering fire serving as a footlight. For all the dangers and distasteful aspects of the mission, Ryerson was enjoying the reunion and their time together in this rugged wilderness.

As if from nowhere, inspiration jabbed into Ryerson's thoughts; a probable answer to their quandary, but risky as hell.

"We've been a pair of fools, Pat," he said.

"Can't speak for you, but I've been one for nigh sixty years. Be specific."

"We've overlooked the obvious."

"On the contrary, my friend, I think we've covered

most of our options. North, south, east, and west. Any way we go from here is pure hell. About all that's left is straight up. Or down."

"Pat, together and separately, we've brought Apaches to bay, and they're the most cunning of all. We call ourselves trackers and scouts. We're supposed to have all this savvy."

"So?"

"The Antrims. It's obvious. If an Apache wanted to stop a pursuer short of killing him—which he'd be most apt to do—what would he do?"

"Disable him, probably. Hamstring most likely. Cut the tendon. Wait a minute! The light dawns. Put them out of commission some way. But how?"

"It's a long walk home, Pat."

"Aha! A horse-thieving patrol by dark of night, by God!"

"Now you're talking like a man with some savvy. There's one more twist that will make sure they won't be around until long after we have Cass and Bonner behind bars."

"I'm stumped again, Cole. How do we do that?"

"Okay, Myles," Ryerson chided. "What does a man walk in?"

"Boots! We also steal their boots. Good play! Damned good play!"

"If we can pull it off."

Graydon was caught up in the idea. "Better give them a few hours to get sound asleep. Mitch is too confident to post a guard. We'll still have to be sneakier than Geronimo himself."

"Right. It's not going to be easy with that trigger-happy bunch. They catch us with our fingers in the pie and we're dead."

"Unless we kill them first. And I'd avoid that at all costs."

"We've both scouted Apaches on the warpath, checked their strength and their positions. That meant sliding by night sentries who were alert as prairie dogs. Smartest by damn fighters in history."

"I left that life eight years ago."

"You saying you aren't man enough, Pat? You forgot how?"

"Not on your old saddle blanket, Boot Hill Cole! As for being man enough, I'm ready when you are, Marshal." Graydon grinned. All day he'd been harassed by thoughts of the Antrims trailing him. He'd been on the defensive. Now, with any kind of luck, he'd be rid of that burr under his saddle and could concentrate on bringing in Bonner and Cass. In the flickering of the fire in front of him, Pat Graydon looked younger to Ryerson.

"We'd better roll up and try to sleep a few hours," Ryerson said. "It's been a long day, and the way we've got it figured, it might not be such an easy night."

"Why, you sick-tailed tinhorn trail dog!" Graydon blurted, the eager smile still spread all over his face. "You set up a patrol like that in my mind, and now you expect me to curl up like a baby just off the tit and go to sleep!"

"Hell, you can stand on your head for a few hours for all I care. Just don't start singing or something because I intend to get some shut-eye."

Ryerson carefully wrapped his spread bedroll around him. Warmly enshrouded in his soogans, he was in the proper position to ease his head back at a comfortable angle against his saddle. He heard Graydon puttering around in the dark across the bed of dimly glowing coals, getting himself tucked in, too.

"Good night, Pat."

"Huh!" Graydon grunted. "You and your big ideas!"

Ryerson sensed that Graydon grinned as he lay his head back and closed his eyes. For a long time Ryerson stared at the velvet forever of the night sky, studying the pinpricks of starlight, so many that they looked like gold dust as he searched for some familiar constellations. It was one of his ways of concentrating on something else, ridding his brain of the tension of the day and what was to come in a few hours.

His mind clear and untroubled, he closed his eyes, trying to recall the nightful of yellow, gemlike points of light in the black depths of an immense dome towering over him. While he was remembering a sky spread with stars, Ryerson drifted away into a pleasant sleep.

The stars were still there, but in a slightly different position, when his eyes opened again. He figured he and Graydon had slept about four hours.

The air had turned colder, and the only sound was the gurgle and chatter of the stream on the other side of the rocks. Water, Ryerson mused as the cobwebs of sleep unsnarled in his head, never rested. Night and day it continued its walk downhill, chatting all the way about where it had been and what it had seen.

"Pat!" he hissed.

"Uh?"

"It's time."

"I'm awake."

They rolled their gear under thin moonlight, to be ready to saddle up when they got back. "Before we go, Pat, let's talk over a battle plan," Ryerson said, his voice husky with sleep. "Mitch won't be savvy enough to post a night watch. He figures we want to stay as far away from them as possible. The last thing he expects is to see us up there—at this time of night."

"And let's hope he doesn't!" Pat joked.

"He ever see any military action, do you know?"

"Naw, I doubt it," Graydon said. "The only night guard he ever pulled was with a bunch of flyblown steers. And that's a far cry from tonight."

"If he does, it'll be him or Mort. They can't trust Myles."

"I wouldn't imagine."

"I might have to take out a man, Pat."

"Don't kill him. We're here to enforce the law, not break it."

"Yes, teacher. I can put a man to sleep so sound he won't wake up till the sun's high. Don't fret."

"Probably they built a big night fire. Should still be a glow to see their camp and to slip in for the boots."

"That's how I figure it."

"You're lighter on your feet and younger and been trackin' scalawags in the *malpais* more lately than me. Believe you'd better go in for the boots, Cole. I'll take on the horses and be ready to back your play, if it comes to that."

"I'll do it quiet. If we can get the horses out of there without waking them, it'd suit me just fine."

"Easy in desert country," Graydon said. "This brush and rocks country is a different matter."

"If they wake up, we fire our guns and make a hullabaloo and hightail it. That'll confuse the hell out of them, particularly just waking up. I'll have the boots, I guarantee it. You make sure you get the horses running."

"From that shot earlier this evenin', I figure them a mile and a half or so north by northeast."

"That still puts them along the stream," Ryerson said. "I'll vote for that. After a mile and a half, we start walking real easy. After two miles we better figure we walked by them and backtrack."

"This old nose'll smell their fire."

"Hell, Pat, figuring their rare exposure to a washtub, I imagine you'll smell something else—particularly since we hope they'll have their boots off!"

Graydon chuckled. "Mitch Antrim's going to shoot me on sight in Patchknife."

"But Bonner and Cass will be behind bars, right?"

"That's all that matters. Let's go!"

"No talking," Ryerson warned. "If we need to confer, we signal first and get close together."

As they had predicted earlier, the moon bathed the land with enough light to see by. Both men had spent years moving cautiously by night and by day. Ryerson's respect for Pat Graydon's scouting abilities was rekindled. The old man moved smoothly and silently as a snake, despite his bulky horseman's boots.

Even in the densely wooded ravines, draws, and creek flats they crossed and moved through, the moon's soft, silvery light gave enough visibility to see obstacles and brush. Moonlight had a way of oozing around everything, leaving only vague shadows. The advantage of such light, along with their conditioned abilities to glide over the land as gently as the wind itself, made the hike a quiet one. But not an easy one. For the most part they moved in silent single file, alternating in the lead. The man ahead spotted the hazards, guiding the other around them or warning of a change in course with hand signals.

Gauging their less-than-regular speed along with the time that had passed, Ryerson tapped Graydon, in the lead, lightly on the shoulder. The burly sheriff eased to a halt. His mouth cupped by his hand, Ryerson bent his head close to Graydon's ear, speaking in such a low whisper he could scarcely hear himself. "Should start smelling wood smoke through here soon. Or feet."

Graydon stifled a chuckle. Ryerson could also see his head bob in agreement.

"Want me to take the lead?" Ryerson whispered.

"You think I've lost my touch?" Graydon quipped, shielding his mouth with his hand close to Ryerson's ear.

"We've come through some mighty rough country in the last hour. If anything, you're better. Just giving you the option."

"You have to make it clear into their camp, Cole. Their horses will be out a ways. You go ahead and lead from here."

Ryerson gingerly stepped around his companion and they moved out, walking even more lightly now, carefully placing their feet to avoid branches or twigs, or slippery streamside stones that could upset a man. Their talk of smelling men first was only a joke. Ryerson's keen nose picked up only the hint of the wood smoke that had drifted laterally on soft night breezes and permeated the air and the trees and the brush around them.

Smoke had a clinging quality to a man used to sensing it, and Ryerson allowed it to guide him as its sharpness increased. As long as it grew strong in his nostrils, he knew he was headed right.

It had been as much as five hours since nightfall when the Antrims rolled up in their soogans. The time since the fire had been fed also affected the aroma and intensity of the smoke, helping Ryerson get a bearing on how far he was from their camp. Old smoke was distinctly different from new smoke. The odors of cooked meat also began to blend with the smoke smell, and Ryerson knew the moment of truth was near.

He smelled and found the horses first. Slight movement in the dark ahead told him that one of the animals had heard them or got a whiff of them. It was not an alarmed movement. It seemed more that a horse became aware of them, swung up his head for a better scent and brushed a low-hanging tree branch.

The Antrims' three horses were hobbled on the flats near the stream's edge where it was grassy. Ryerson stopped, turning to Graydon and signaling. Graydon returned the sign of understanding in the murky moonlight. He slid silently toward the animals, approaching them with a practiced caution, but with an ease and assurance in his manner that kept the horses off guard and calm. Pat's glide over the uneven ground was so slick, Ryerson couldn't make out a sound.

Away from the stream, toward a higher bank, his

sharp eyes caught through the night the glow of a bed of embers. In the moonlight a single strand of smoke trailed up as a ghostly pillar into the untroubled night air. Now he moved so lightly that only the soles of his boots caressed the earth and rocks. He'd have given anything for his soft Apache moccasins, left in New Mexico.

The Antrims had been here long enough to have beaten something of a path from their camp to the horses and the stream. The heavyweight trio had done a good job of tramping down any brittle twigs Ryerson might encounter. With an expert glide he eased closer to where they lay. The three sleeping bodies were bulked under blankets that had wrinkled and pulled up and twisted in the night. From the size, he identified Mitch and Mort, still reasonably well covered. Myles, lying with arms and legs outstretched, was a contorted sleeping shape, the length of blanket pulled up and rolled and twisted and covering only his chest and belly. Myles didn't snore, but Ryerson could hear the raspy intake of his breathing.

These men had a great deal to learn about tucking in a bedroll, Ryerson thought; but then, they had a lot to learn—and they'd learn much of it along about daylight when reality also dawned on them. Ryerson grinned into the night.

From the inert mound he identified as Mitch, a regular and guttural snore issued, resounding in the open space between the trees of their camp. If the snoring stopped, Ryerson was prepared to freeze in place, maybe go for his gun. Blending with a tree close to the sleeping trio, he studied the situation. Myles had gone to sleep wearing his boots; Mitch and Mort had pulled theirs off. Ryerson tallied his alternatives. Myles was some smaller than his brothers, and it was doubtful if even his twin could fit into his boots to forge ahead for help when, in the morning, they angrily started covering the miles home in stockinged feet.

Despite his concentration on stealth, Ryerson couldn't stifle another grin as his mind's ear heard the howls and the mule-skinner language when the Antrims would find they'd been taken for fools. Better not dally, he told himself. Get Mitch and Mort's boots and get away from here with all speed. Crouching low, he edged toward the sleeping men. He had tiptoed between Mort and Mitch and was about to stoop for the boots when Mitch's snore stopped abruptly and he thrashed in his blankets.

Tensely, his breath stopped in his throat, Ryerson waited, ready to swing up his gun. Mitch grumbled something, twitched once and again lay quietly. Ryerson could hear mucous again rattling in Mitch's head as his snoring resumed.

Ryerson bent gingerly, keeping his eyes on Mitch, making sure he had a firm grip on the boots. He backed away from the sleepers, turned and pussyfooted to where Pat waited. When he approached the flat area of the creek bank and the distinctive and acrid smell of fresh dung, the horses were gone. Graydon was out ahead of him somewhere, leading the animals back toward their camp.

Breathing easier, Ryerson still walked softly, carrying the boots, turning southward through the night, following now the scent of dried animal sweat and horseflesh. He quickly overtook the rear animal and hurried to the head of the line where Graydon trudged, leading them. They shook hands in jubilation.

"Well, I see you got the clodhoppers," Graydon whispered, jubilation tinkling in his voice.

"All but Myles's. Wouldn't you know, he went to sleep wearing them. But you got the bigger game. I never heard a thing, and I was listening."

"Your ears ain't what a lawman's ought to be, Mr. Ryerson."

"What are you talking about, Pat?"

"Them damned beans, son. I was about ready to head out with these cayuses when I got an uncommon urge to fart. A regular old gut buster."

"Did you?"

"You didn't hear?"

"Uh-uh."

"Then I guess you'll never know."

Chuckling, Pat Graydon reefed on his lead rope and charged off into the darkness.

⇒ 6 ⇐

In the night, they strung the captured horses together like beads and led them along when they moved out from their campsite, heading south again.

"No sense in just turning them loose," Graydon advised, "or all our work would be for naught. They'd probably be smart enough to turn back north, the Antrims would catch them quicker'n scat and be on our back trail in no time, painted for war."

"And really out for blood this time."

Graydon looked at Ryerson in the dim light, eyes rolling in acknowledgment. It had taken them most of the night to get back to their camp in the dark, slowed by the horses. Dawn broke around them with a kind of gray flush bleeding out of the sky to the east, a cold sort of false light. They could see enough to make their final preparations to ride on after Cass and Bonner.

Ryerson had tied his bedroll and other belongings behind his saddle and was up, holding the lead rope to their unwanted remuda. The big, loose-built Graydon hoisted himself heavily onto his horse with a kind of stifled grunt.

"Don't you be looking at me, Mr. Ryerson," he said. "I'll be all right."

Ryerson responded by nudging his horse into a walk, still following the stream bed, hearing Graydon's cluck behind him and the movement of his mount as he made his way around the string of horses and moved ahead to the point position.

"By full day we'll be out of this," he said as he guided his horse over rough ground past Ryerson. They rode wordlessly for an hour, with the world taking shape around them.

True to Graydon's word, as daylight pushed away the last vestiges of night, the land turned easier to move through. With the coming of full light, the gray giving way to blue in the sky, Ryerson saw it, the country they would ride down. Ahead of them it leveled off to roll away to an infinity of miles of prairie, dipping and plunging and rearing up to low hills. It went on even beyond the knolls, limited only by a man's vision, pouring itself into the sky at the boundaries of sight. The air turned so bright and clear, it appeared to Ryerson that he might count the trees and blades of grass sprouting at the very farthest reach of his eyes.

The captured horses consented willingly to being led, a blessing in itself. They probably appreciated traveling without their accustomed heavy loads, Ryerson thought, and commanding spurs and slaps. If they had turned balky, it would have slowed them down, and Ryerson knew that Graydon hoped to have Cass and Bonner in custody by nightfall. They'd have to make tracks, and it was good that the land had turned easier to move through and that the extra horses were cooperative.

It was also a blessing in disguise that they'd have the extra mounts in case their own horses grew tired.

Graydon eased his pace to let Ryerson ride up alongside as they became buried in the immensity of the land. To the west the mountains stood on hind legs like great craggy pyramids crowding shoulder to shoulder, bulky at the base to rise raggedly against the sky. Snow still clung in patches at their summits and streamed fingerlike down canyons and clefts close to the peaks. Around the two riders and their remuda, the sun rose swiftly, painting the land with a yellowness soft as candle flame. But a wind was up here, too, drumming at them gently then suddenly pushy, reminding them with chill gusts that night was not that long past.

"I see some sign along here that we must be on the right track," Graydon called over his shoulder, his face wrinkling in a smile of optimism. "Grass is bent here and there, and enough to look like two animals did it." His voice took on the teacher tone Ryerson remembered fondly from their joint expeditions in the desert country north of the line. Ryerson grinned, anticipating Graydon's next remark. He said it every time.

"A man's foot'll bend the grass ahead. A horse's hoofs'll swing up and back, pointing back the way he came."

"Bet you missed that stack of horse turds back there a ways, Pat," Ryerson said.

"Didn't," Graydon said with a mock superior air. "Dropped yesterday. We're slidin' the groove, son, sure as I'm a foot high. The creek moved off way east of here after we left that rough country, so they must've gone into a dry camp somewhere up ahead. There's some springs and waterin' holes in through here, but so few and far between they wouldn't know 'em or how to find 'em. They probably still have some whiskey with them, so short of bathin', which I figure they're not long on to begin with, they got no great need of water. I don't imagine either of them cares a damn about a horse. They'll remember to water them when they come across it somewhere."

"I don't know this country at all, Pat, but it appears they're making good time."

"Ain't lollygaggin' and that's for sure. We ought to strike their night camp place before noon if I'm any judge. Then all we got to do is eat up the country between there and where they plan to bed down tonight. I still want them to spend this night roped together and eating our beans!"

"You make it sound easy."

"Don't I wish! The Antrim boys didn't expect us to be up their way, so we pulled things off slick last night. Bonner and Cass are running for their necks and doing nothing but looking back over their shoulders watching for us. I'd sure like to catch them napping the way we did the Antrims."

"The element of surprise and the night would be in our favor again."

"I sure don't relish them seeing us out in the open and making a run for it. No doubt we could catch up, but there could be gunplay and all sorts of nasty things could happen."

"It may anyway, Pat. As I see it, they know they're running from the hangman for sure as it is. No jury in the world's going to acquit that pair, and particularly not in Patchknife."

"Matt Antrim wasn't the most beloved man in the basin, Cole, but in this case, fortune favors fools, meaning our Mr. Cass and Mr. Bonner. By the way, son, it's good sense to plan ahead. You don't know this country. If anything goes haywire, the stage road is about thirty miles west, in through the foothills. The country's about as easy that way as this, until you get to the mountains."

"The stage road comes before the mountains, then?"

"Right. Tom Moon Dog's place is on it, north a little by west of where we are right now."

"That's good to know."

"Look, Cole. Out south. That bunch of trees coming up there. There'll be water near the surface, maybe even a spring. I'd bet my spurs we'll find where Cass and Bonner spent the night."

"Looks like it might even be a buffalo wallow," Ryerson said. "And you said there was nothing but jackrabbits out here."

"You know how I stretch things, Cole. I haven't been out here in a while. I didn't think the game would be this thick."

Ryerson had seen evidence of buffalo this way, the sighting of chips more frequent as they approached the cluster of trees where Graydon figured they'd come onto Bonner and Cass's night camp. The concentrated droppings suggested something that tended to keep the buffalo in this neighborhood, like a mudhole wallow.

At this distance he could make out whip-thin aspens, their veins of branches thick with spadelike leaves, their silvery undersides performing a nervous flickering dance in the breezes coming down from the western range. Sycamores were here, too, showing bulkier and white, their trunks dappled with scabby and dead, gray-brown bark.

Through the morning, Ryerson had seen in the great distances the ragged clusters of ranging buffalo like heaps of dark rock, their massive brown heads down, beards brushing the ground as they browsed, high shaggy humps towering over the huge beasts as they moved in a snail's pace in their grazing. Buffalo herds had dwindled in the West, but though the hide hunters had made a dent in the once-great herds, he thought, they still had a job of work ahead to eliminate them all.

He'd seen antelope, too, small bands, spooking when they saw the men on horseback, darting off with graceful bounce to flow and fade into the distance like brittle leaves driven before the wind.

Ryerson and Graydon got down at the clump of trees to rest the horses and to check the spot. Bonner and Cass had been there, judging from the ashes in another recent fire ring. The pair had left some of their hauled-in buffalo chips and broken lengths of sycamore limbs to stoke their night fire.

"Even though they're running scared, Pat, they're not doing much to cover their tracks," Ryerson said.

"Not slick enough to, son. I give them four, at the most five hours head start on us." Graydon glanced at the sky. "I told you noon, and I was close to right. So far, things are running in our favor."

Ryerson glanced up, seeing the sun diffused through the web of sycamore leaves directly over him. "I don't see four or five more hours of solid riding much of a favor, Pat."

"Well, hell, look on the bright side, Cole. We've shaken the Antrims off our tails, at least for now. We've tracked Cass and Bonner as true as if we were hounds to the scent. We'll take a breather for something to eat. Have us some jerky and cold beans if you want. We'll lollygag here awhile, give the horses a rest, and move out slow. I'd still rather catch them in the night camp. Go in after they're asleep, like we did Mitch and them last night."

Away from the trees, a mudhole lay like a dimple in the earth, with the grass rubbed away from it for yards around by buffalo, showing where a spring seeped lazily out of the ground.

As if he had nothing better to do, Graydon made for the open space to work the kinks out, walking stiff and uneven from the morning hours on horseback. Ryerson, resting against a tree trunk, watched him go through slitted eyes, enjoying the few moments of relaxation.

The sudden sounds came one after the other—a slapping thump, a gasped grunt of surprise or pain or both, and the crack of a distant rifle. The roaring report died quickly, with nothing to echo against as the breezes tossed it away. Pat Graydon lurched and fell, landing at the mudhole's edge, a thrashing, jerking bundle of arms and legs getting dusty from the powdery stuff the buffalo had churned up.

Despite a jab of shock and surprise, Ryerson reacted with conditioned coolness. Instinctively and like a tiny animal, he darted for cover, Colt Navy cocked and ready when he hit the protecting base of the nearest sycamore.

All was quiet but for the wind moving fitfully over him, making a soft kind of moan as it combed the lacing of leaves and limbs. It was a lonely, depressing kind of sound, since just now it was the only sound there was.

Ryerson peered out from cover, his chest tight, his heart hammering a choked constricting pulse in his dry throat. In wide-eyed disbelief he watched as, a mere thirty yards away, the rounded hulk of Pat Graydon's body twitched and convulsed at the edge of the wallow, part of him already muddy from it.

His mind tearing at the enormity of what had happened, Ryerson weighed the wisdom of making a dash for Pat's body to bring him in, to see how badly he was hurt. But someone was out there, probably Bonner and Cass, having set up a perfect dry-gulch for two supposedly seasoned trackers. Ryerson's head ached with the stupidity of being led into an ambush like a rabbit to the snare. He gritted his teeth and locked his eyelids in fury and grief. What a hell of a thing to have happen, he thought angrily. His best friend lay dying, and there was nothing he could do. If he appeared in the open, there was a bullet out there with his name on it.

Graydon lay still now, within Ryerson's sight, enough in the open to be too risky to get to. It had accidentally become a well-set trap for Ryerson as well, with the body of Graydon, dead or alive, as bait.

Ryerson twisted himself around to see the four horses hooked together a hundred yards away on the prairie, grazing again, quieting after the gun blast shattered the silence. Graydon's animal was close to Ryerson's. The three Antrim ponies stood spooked and skittish, heads up, the ends of their ropes tied to Ryerson's saddle. Ryerson only hoped that when he'd gotten down, he had the tethers secured.

Myles had failed to take off his saddle the night before, and from his saddle horn dangled two pairs of well-worn range boots.

Ryerson came alert to the quick, measured beat of hoofs drumming on the land, muffled by the distance and the rolling country, but coming louder to his ears. South of the grove two big men on small galloping horses rose out of a grassy hollow and spurred their horses to where Ryerson and Graydon's string now stopped cropping to look up, startled by the sudden appearance of the two mounted men.

Cass and Bonner had planned their moves well, to be out of pistol range, sensing that the Winchesters of the two lawmen would be safely booted on their saddles. Knowing they moved too fast and too far away for any effective shooting, Ryerson still leaped into the open as the pair neared the five riderless horses, splitting around them as they went, hazing them into motion with whoops and whistles.

Ryerson's stomach, heart, and lungs were squeezed bags of fury and frustration as he bent on one knee, cupped his Navy in both hands and laid a pair of rounds at the retreating pair. They were big enough to make good targets, but the range was impossible.

One of them spun in the saddle to return the fire, clumsily succeeding only in putting his bullet between the eyes of Myles Antrim's horse, galloping behind him in the pack of spooked animals. The horse collapsed on flailing legs and in a flurry of churned dust to slam on its side onto the hard-packed dirt. Seized with opportunity, Ryerson sprinted for it; there'd be a loaded Winchester in the saddle boot. He'd have the advantage again!

At the dead animal, Ryerson skidded and dropped in one easy braking motion to tug at a gun's thick butt stock jutting from under the inert horse. Ferociously he wrenched at the weapon imprisoned under dead weight, feeling it gradually yield. With agonizing slowness the shotgun of the dim-wit Antrim emerged. The pair of thin barrels had flattened and bent with the impact of the horse's fall.

Furious but undaunted, Ryerson hurled it away from him in bitter disgust; he dropped instinctively behind the horse to protect himself and to empty his Navy at the retreating pair, resting it for stability against the dead animal's steaming ribs. It was futile.

Neither Bonner nor Cass fired again. They were obscured in the screen of their own dust, defying his marksmanship, their floppy hat brims bucked up at the front against the wind, their poorly tied duffel flopping behind their saddles. They were big men in similar clothing, as much alike as the Antrim twins.

Ryerson's frenzied four remaining pistol shots were barks that darted away abruptly on the flat, cutting prairie wind as he touched off his rounds, taking a fine sight over the Navy's hammer notch. He aimed keen on their retreating backs, correcting for windage and elevation for an arcing trajectory, pleading with God to allow him to knock one of them out of the saddle.

He watched his rounds harmlessly cuff the dust behind the flying hooves of the killers' horses. Then they were out of sight in the hills and hollows of grass and their puffs of dust. Everything turned quiet and tight. Only the moan was there in the leaves and limbs behind him, the wail of a disconsolate wind. Ryerson could have wished for happier sounds.

He knelt for a long moment on the ground, head

down in defeat, the empty Navy at his side, trembling in this moment of collapse and horror at the sudden events of a few minutes, desperately struggling to regain his breath and his composure. Abruptly, he glanced at Pat Graydon's body, some distance away. Pat hadn't moved.

The weight of it all descended on Ryerson; his best friend was dead. Powder and ball for his Navy were on his rustled horse; the only other available horse was useless, as was the only available long-arm, young Antrim's shotgun. Ryerson spit into the dirt in disgust and defeat, and trudged dejectedly to Graydon's body.

The dead man lay face down, pulled and twisted from the impact, a hulking jumble of arms and legs, torso and clothing. His hat had sailed away, and now the ground wind combed eerily through his hair with needlelike fingers; Pat's hair looked dismally gray and shockingly dead.

A gaping hole had been blown through the back of his shirt and vest from the soft lead that had flattened as it plowed through Pat's vital organs. Some blood, torn flesh, and shattered bone oozed around the exit wound. Ryerson felt his reserves of vitality and will purge themselves through his fingers and toes. His body felt emptied, the void filled with a bitter acid of anguish and anger—that he had been so stupid, and that as a result a precious friend was gone and he himself was stranded in a hostile wilderness in a land he knew little about.

He tenderly rolled Graydon over to move him away from the mud, powerless to do anything else for an old friend. He shuddered with the enormity of it all. Walking out of the grove, Graydon had taken the shot head-on, square in the chest. He probably hadn't so much as heard it.

Graydon's face, splattered with mud and sprinkled with dust as he went down, had an expression of complete surprise frozen into it.

7

Ryerson knelt and tried to gently scoop the battered body into his arms. It was no use; Graydon was too heavy. He worked his arms under the man's shoulders to lift him from the waist. He dragged the body, sliding slack and dead, into the open area of the grove. As tenderly as possible, Ryerson gently stretched Graydon out in a comfortable-looking position, as if it mattered. At least it mattered to the living, he thought.

He took off Graydon's gun belt, rolled the holstered gun into it and put it where he'd be sure to remember it when he came to leave. He walked, stoop-shouldered in defeat, to the mudhole and picked up Pat's dust-spattered tan Stetson, remembering with moist eyes how Graydon wore it square to his head, proudly. Taking the hat, he walked back, his mind hardly on what he was doing. With his bandanna he did his best to clean the mud off the dead face. The aging, lined, and weather-pitted flesh of the old features responded to his massaging as though the man who owned them was still alive. Ryerson half expected Graydon to open his eyes and say, "Hey, not so rough there, son!"

It was nasty, distasteful work, but Ryerson did it

anyway, the least he could do under the circumstances. When he had cleaned the face as best he could, he studied it for a long time from his kneeling position beside the body, remembering a friendship that had been strengthened and tempered in a crucible of challenge, adventure, and comradeship.

Awareness of his plight crept into Ryerson's thoughts; with a sigh he set them aside to consider what he would be able to do for his dead friend. He looked again at Graydon's face.

The expression of surprise that had frozen in the features at death had softened, and the old scout seemed only to sleep peacefully.

Ryerson walked to a sycamore to slump against its trunk, his rump uncomfortably rammed against its roots as he regarded the body from across the fire ring. The relaxed form was that of a man having a short siesta before getting back into the saddle to ride on to whatever mission had brought him into this forsaken land in the first place.

Ryerson closed his eyes, emotionally exhausted, and for several minutes his mind lurked at the borders of sleep. In that limbo, a near-dream persuaded him that all this had not happened and that Pat, indeed, was merely having a short snooze. Ryerson opened his eyes, only to have the shock of reality again hit him with express-train impact.

Though he had long ago made a pact with himself to never say die no matter how badly the cards ran against him, he felt a rising frustration and childish anger welling up in him, and felt the bitter sting of restrained tears around his eyelids.

Blinking against the moisture, he closed his eyes again, this time not to retreat from reality, but to try to come to grips with it. Thoughts and memories swirled together, a composite of then and now emerging to help make these terrifying first moments tolerable and to remind him that he had found strength to move on after the other tragedies of his life.

His thoughts were not good ones, nor were they easy, happy thoughts and memories. Soldiering and lawkeeping were alike in that regard; a man found his friends among those dedicated and good at what they did, and, like him, savored the sting and clash of combat if it was war, or challenge, if it was enforcing the law.

Bereft of options in a strange land, with calamity his sudden companion as well as behind him and ahead of him and, it seemed, all around him, Ryerson's mind's eye re-created the figure of redheaded, handsome and cocksure, enduringly loyal Confederate Captain Dan Sturgis taking the Yankee cavalryman's saber thrust intended for Ryerson himself.

And the bitter memory of loves lost over his pigheadedness in battling for causes; Ruth Bascom Sturgis, his first-ever love, a respectable widowhood passed, declining his offer of marriage by refusing to risk a new commitment threatened by the grief of another loss to the sword or the gun.

Another spunky redhead remembered—Ruby Montez, young and troubled, but strong underneath, in Ryerson's mind combining the best he had found in both Dan and Ruth Sturgis; his and Ruby's fondness for each other was allowed mere days to build and mellow before Ruby's tragic loss to a raging river in hasty flight from the clutches of an evil rustler chieftain.

Opening his misty eyes, Ryerson looked around him and again at Pat's body, relaxed in death across the fire ring, a hint of composure beginning to settle over his thoughts. Now, he reasoned, he must come to grips with reality. He was alone in a land he had little in common with; somewhere to the north, three furious Antrims were hoofing it in bare feet back to their ranch for remounts. They were ready to kill him before for interfering. Now he had seriously interfered, and when they found him, it would be an immediate three against one in a gunfight, no quarter given, no negotiating.

Afoot now himself, he would be fair game when the Antrims found him. They'd track him down, kill without emotion and continue on to the capture and lynching of Sam Cass and Lacey Bonner. His mind's ear tuned to Myles Antrim's whiny but eager, half-wit voice: "We—We gonna hang 'em up by they heels an'—an' I git to built a fa'r under they heads!"

And now the pair destined for that kind of inglorious and slow death galloped southward with Ryerson's only ready means of escape or pursuit. His mind clear and seized with reality, Ryerson sifted his alternatives. He owed it to Pat Graydon to forge on south and do his best to bring in Cass and Bonner. On foot? A virtual impossibility. Even if he walked day and night, they'd still stay ahead by days that would grow into weeks.

His mind shouted "absurd," but second thoughts asked what outs he had left. In any walk back to Patchknife, he faced an ordeal of about fifty miles. Moon Dog's stage station was off there somewhere under the mountains' rim, Lord knew where, their lofty prominence the source of that ever-present hum of wind that seemed bent on harassing him. It swung again through the limbs and leaves over him, whipping the branches ever so slightly whenever it took the notion, letting up a bit and then starting in again, seeming to be there solely to drive a harried man to distraction when he had enough other vexations on his mind.

Ryerson sensed himself getting edgy over something he couldn't control—like the wind—and that was no good. He needed his energies for the things he could cope with. It was time, he thought, to take stock of things he could control. Pat Graydon's body had to be dealt with. Without burial of some sort, the body would be attacked overnight by wolves and other scavengers that fed off carrion, and by morning would be a shambles. Ryerson's mind could not tolerate such a thought.

A cairn of rocks! "That's it," Ryerson said aloud, his voice ringing in the stillness. "I'll take the time to haul in rocks and pile them around him." It wasn't the best, but that way the hounds of hell could not touch the body. His mind turned busy with the task, and for the time of strenuous work, he forgot his desperate straits. Again and again he plodded out into the prairie for stones, heaving at some of them to pry them loose from their primordial resting places, lugging in the large ones to form an oval ring close to the body. It was tough, grueling work.

He had hauled in only a third enough rocks for a satisfactory job of permanently cloaking the body. Ryerson was soaked with sweat. His mouth was tight and sour from dryness, with no means of slaking a maddening thirst. The moisture of the mudhole was too laced with dirt and hair and dung to drink. His legs and back cramped and ached from his effort. He tried chewing grass to take moisture from it, but its bitter, astringent taste puckered the insides of his mouth. He spit out the green mash in disgust.

To rest and relieve his aching muscles, he braved the glaring sun again for a long walk in the direction from which the rifle shot had come and the point where Bonner and Cass first galloped into sight. He strode boldly, hands shoved into hip pockets, trying for the moment to forget his grisly mission in the grove.

The signs he found showed that they had lurked there since dawn. Their horses had grazed, trampling and chewing in a wide area in the grassy bowl below where the outlaws lay in ambush. The pocket in the land was also scattered with dumpings from the horses; a man had similarly relieved himself. The latter sight disgusted him.

His mind troubled and centering on the awful catastrophe of Graydon's brutal death, Ryerson climbed to the rim of the bowl where it faced the grove and mud wallow. At the edge, the grass was matted and crushed where the men had lain a long time waiting, anticipating their prey. An ejected .44 Winchester casing lay nearby, the one obviously kicked out of the breech and a fresh one levered in after Graydon was killed.

He picked up the casing, smelling at its circle of brass neck the familiar odor of spent powder. He studied it, thinking how it stood for stupidity on the part of two seasoned trackers who should have known better and should have been on their guard against such a depraved attack.

Ryerson uttered a disgusted "Shit!" He distractedly dropped the shell into his shirt pocket and went back to hunting for rocks closer to the mudhole.

By late afternoon, totally spent and feeling a gnawing hunger griping in the pit of his stomach, his mouth and throat withered in a fiery thirst, Ryerson had hauled in enough rocks for his cairn and had totally encased the body under the pile. He used his small stones to fill any gaps around the large boulders.

As he worked, Ryerson loathed this grove of death and ached for his taxing chore to be finished; yet he would not relent until all was proper. Taking off his hat and mopping his flowing forehead with his sleeve, he walked into the open prairie, hopeful of a cooling breeze. Movement in the sky over him caught his attention; the word was out. Already a buzzard circled the grove, riding the updrafts light as a wafer of brittle leaf rides a stream, not flapping its wings, but keeping a wide, soaring circle, gently rolling its body with wings outstretched and delicately tipped to take advantage of moving currents way up there.

"Come ahead, you bastard!" Ryerson yelled furiously through gritted teeth, a choked sob in his voice, angrily shaking a clenched fist at the heavens. "You'll not touch him now!" The sun lowered itself toward the jagged peaks, burning his eyes as he faced it and it made ready to slide down behind the range and again bring darkness to the land and the grove and his massive burial vault for Pat Graydon. Already the dark was thick in there as the trees sucked away the last of the evening light and filled the spaces with a depressing twilight.

Ryerson dragged himself back into the grove for the last time, remembering the man, the friend of long and good years, who lay under the stones. Ryerson's tone was softer now, almost hoarse. "I'm sorry, Pat. Should have used better judgment. Sorry it had to end this way. I did what I could for you. But I'll see the rest of the job through better than this. As best I can, I'll see it through. That's my word."

With the saying of it, Ryerson knew he had tossed aside his other choices—walking back to Patchknife, or the shorter route to Tom Moon Dog's stage station. Now it was root hog or die. Head south. Walk night and day if that's what it took. Forget that Cass and Bonner had brutally murdered Matt and Stella Antrim. Remember only that they had killed Pat Graydon in a dirty, low-down ambush, never giving the kindhearted sheriff a chance. That was enough.

Ryerson had thought it through, and made his pact with the dead. Despite the odds against him, he'd bring in Cass and Bonner. He looked around the grove again as it lost form in the gathering night. He was hungry, thirsty, and tired. Yet the need for revenge boiled inside him, driving him with renewed energy. He would seek his vengeance for the body that lay under his pile of dirt-scabbed stones, a monument that called for the men who did it to repay. Repay, dammit, Ryerson's mind shouted. *Repay!*

Ryerson took one last, longing look at his cairn.

"I'll be back, Pat," he said softly. "I'll be back and bring in more rocks for the right kind of place for you. I'll see there's a proper monument, too. I'll be back."

Driven by that vow, Ryerson slammed his hat squarely on his head the way Graydon liked to wear his, and buckled the dead sheriff's gun belt across his own with the holster to the left, the grip facing out. He strode boldly away from the grove with an objective now, squinting at the dying light to the west. He swung south with a determined stride and began his walk.

The evening's coming chill already probed inside his thin shirt with cold fingers. His heavy trail coat was rolled in his soogans behind his horse's saddle. And that horse was off somewhere to the south, being tugged along with the others by Cass and Bonner. They would be little worried about that, Ryerson mused; horse-thieving was the least of their concerns.

The loss of his horse and belongings, in themselves, angered him, though, and that anger warmed him as he stepped up his pace, feeling better to be moving again and that the good-byes had been said to Pat Graydon. His lungs filled and his heart pumped renewed vitality into his system. His concern about hunger and thirst diminished. There was something, he consoled himself, about taking a direct hit such as life had just given him, and getting up, shaking off the pain and the humiliation and starting off again. A cause larger than himself was a good thing to have, he thought, and in a strange way, he thanked Pat Graydon for presenting it. The worst wasn't all that bad once it had happened and a man came to grips with it and determined his course. Now it was plant one foot ahead of the other and forge onward.

As he walked, feeling warmth returning in his moving blood, the sun let itself at last down behind the far hills and slid away from them; it floated off into oblivion beyond the ragged peaks, and an even deeper stillness came over the vast land facing him. The stark reality of silence emphasized the futility of his mission. Yet in his mind determination remained; root hog or die.

Behind him the buzzard tightened its soaring circle in the fading light, drifting closer to earth to land undisturbed, to check on the feast that seemed waiting under the trees.

Within but a few minutes the low-flying scavenger and the grove were lost to sight in the immense stretch of darkening land behind Ryerson. With the mountains as his guide, he kept them over his right shoulder, moving ever southward. If he couldn't follow the track of Cass and Bonner and the horses after dark, he could continue on this course and, come daylight, zigzag over the land until he was again on their trail.

Something would come up. He'd find a stream to refresh his parched body; somehow he'd find something to eat. Assuring himself of these good objectives, Ryerson trudged the land for an hour as it lay in twilight, a dimness that grew deeper and grayer as he went, but light enough to see where he put his feet and giving him enough landmarks to keep his bearings.

The euphoria of his start was short-lived. As his system settled into the routine, fatigue, thirst, and hunger became acute. It was a time of concentrating on his goal and getting angry again; it would be a nasty business, walking down Cass and Bonner while they made twice his time from horseback. No matter; he gave himself orders like the former captain of cavalry that he was. Dress up your line! Straighten up! Shoulders back! Chin up! Remember the enemy and the cause you fight for!

The cause was back there in the silent clay that had been Pat Graydon. Ryerson knew if he was to pull through, he'd have to will it. He'd, by God, bring justice to Pat Graydon's killers if he had to ride shank's mare clear to Texas. Something would break in his favor before then.

As he walked, forcing a confident, carefree stride, he worked at a reverse draw of Graydon's six-gun with his left hand; the weapon was hung and tied to his left hip at a convenient level. Again and again as he went along, his footsteps beating a military cadence on the hard-packed land, Ryerson flipped his hand back in a cuffing motion, swiveling his wrist, sliding the weapon smoothly out of the holster, pivoting it up, thumbing the hammer back as he did. Gradually as he practiced, his retrieval of the gun became faster. He began working at drawing the six-gun and his useless Colt Navy together.

Darkness deepened around him, but it was no matter. He could see well enough to walk. The gun practice kept his mind off his physical and emotional exhaustion.

Again he quickened his lagging steps, shelving hunger and thirst; instead of being tempted to concentrate on an abundance of cool water and ample food waiting for him somewhere, it was Bonner and Cass he forced into his eyes as now he skillfully brought up the two guns as swiftly as the dart of a snake's tongue.

When at last he confronted them, he would have the edge on two men at once. He calculated on it. With a nighttime of practice, he would quickly become the equal of the two of them.

Mental images were a fine means of pushing reality aside. He had already seen them once, when they galloped out of the swale outside the grove. They were huge, hulking brutes—he had seen that—and in his head he conjured their faces up close. Their faces were mean, vicious, ugly, a splendid spur to a man seeking to right an awful wrong.

He was there now, in his head, facing them in a camp as they went for their guns. Lightning-fast, he pulled his two guns—physically he did it again—and had them at bay, the hammers smoothly clicking to full cock. Already Graydon's cartridge gun felt comfortable in his left hand, and he felt sure of its aim; close quarters didn't demand a fine sight.

The moon emerged, immense and orange off the ragged horizon to the east. Ryerson took a breather and studied it as it blocked out much of the sky to his right, looming large, a great wafer of fire over the vast and rolling prairie country. Slowly it seeped up, exposing more of itself, growing smaller in the sky, all the time casting more light on the land.

After a long twilight the land had gone dark, but now, reflected brilliance from a sun long since gone to bed painted the moon to drop its light around him, dimly defining every blade of grass, every rock and ripple in the land, every feature. Only in the distance did it dim away to pitch-dark, and Ryerson knew that when he got there, he would be able to define things. Walk, man, walk, he urged himself, commanding his vitality to stay with him as each step brought him closer to Bonner and Cass. Relentlessly, Cole Ryerson trudged on.

Out of the corner of his right eye, he saw a ribbon of moonlight begin to take shape, regular and dependable, coming at his line of travel at a sharp angle; a wagon trail coming down from the northwest. Swiftly he walked to the vee where it merged with his planned route. Two vague ruts cut the land, moving as he was, ever southward. They were too indistinct and overgrown to be the stage road, and certainly not where he expected to find it. Nevertheless, it was a wagon track.

It would lead to human habitation where he'd find water, maybe food and relief. There, also, he might find Sam Cass and Lacey Bonner. That thought was unsettling in his weakened condition, but it would bring his quest quickly to a head.

His mind giddy with fatigue, Ryerson paused to build his strength. He crouched, resting, his eyes busy and intent as they combed the grass around him for sign. It was lightly bent here and there, the blades pointing southward, some of the grass flung and crushed backward in the direction of the little used wagon road. Pat Graydon's well-worn advice about the differences in men and horses bending the grass rang in his head, bringing a wave of depression. Ryerson got up, squared his shoulders and trudged on.

Again he studied the sky and a moon growing small as it climbed its unseen nightly ladder. By the clock it would still be evening. The road veered south, and he set his booted feet in its ruts and forged ahead.

Behind him, surely, this trail would merge with the stage road and, ultimately, at Tom Moon Dog's stage station. It was good to know.

Ryerson had his bearings. In the moonlight the mountains lifted black and bulky against the nighttime sky, their sawtooth profile blocking out a part of the heavens and the myriad stars that began to wink to life.

Practicing his two-handed draw as he walked, Ryerson wondered at the road he was on and where it led, content that its southbound twists and curls led him ever closer to his quarry.

His vow to Pat Graydon's body rang in his ears, now expressed in even stronger terms and spurring him on.

"I'll bring the sons of bitches to justice, Pat. You can depend on that!"

8

The land around him slept softly through the night like a mighty giant. The moon continued its arcing duty across the heavens, always prominent in the black canopy over Ryerson, an ebony infinity pricked with the fine dusting of stars, so many as to take a man's breath away just thinking about the multitude of them as they, too, kept their nightly vigil over a sleeping land.

Even as he stared ahead, the stars were there, riding down the night sky to the far reaches of a limitless horizon.

Still, like a tiny ant buried in the nothingness of a forever land, Cole Ryerson trudged on. The wagon road wormed its way ever southward; surely, he thought, Bonner and Cass had followed this easy transit over the land. He had seen where they and their string of captured horses had joined it.

Sometimes the road veered and twisted like a frightened, tortured thing away from and around obstacles on the land, always coming back on center like a compass needle pointing south.

For a long time the road flowed gracefully downward to lead him at last into a deep canyon with sloping walls towering into the night over the man afoot.

His steps worked along the ancient gravel of a long-dead stream bed, grinding and gritty under his boot soles. Maybe in spring or with heavy rains, water ran through here. Now it was dry. The roadbed was tamped and hard in the wagon ruts, and he made better time on it without the grassy hummock of center strip to walk beside or straddle awkwardly.

When the canyon dwindled, the shallow mouth of it veered away to his right, moving westward. The wagon road climbed out of the cleft in the land slowly, snaking again as it went, until Ryerson found himself back in the broad, high plains country. The twisty ribbon was again marked by the high band of grass between ruts worn by wagon wheels.

Ryerson lost all track of time and distance. He could have come five miles or he could have come ten. Like a man half conscious, he plodded out those miles, his mind open and empty, his eyes centering on where he put his feet and on the awesome land stretching before him.

Only the moon, intent on its course through the heavens, gave him any indication that the hour was on early morning. The miles lay out there, bathed in the moon's dull pewter silver, painting the exhausting vastness, constantly emphasizing the futility of his quest.

He trudged up a slope and crested the top of a slow rolling hill. Below him on a broad and flat expanse of land, a bar of bright yellow broke the dimness of the moonlight, jutting from something dark and bulky but with regular lines. Ryerson rubbed his exhausted eyes and shook his frame as he analyzed the scene below. Some distance from the shining light was another bulking shape—a mere clot of form in the dark with no bar of yellow showing from it. His breath caught in his throat, and Ryerson tried to concentrate his fatigue-fogged brain on the scene.

A ranch, maybe. The other form could be a small stable or barn. The light must come from lamps inside a cabin, the glow coming through an open door. Cautiously he started a quiet, probing walk down the slope toward the flat spread of ranch yard. As he neared the flats he became aware that a stream emerged from somewhere and twisted its snaky ditch along the base of the hill. He could hear its soft, slithering sound in the dark, and feel that the air was colder as he approached it. He silently flexed his arms and hands. This was no time for the cold to render him clumsy. Anything could happen in the next few minutes.

The wagon road led him to a wood bridge over the stream, two enormous cross beams overlaid with thick planking. He walked it softly, making certain his boots did not thud on the bridge flooring.

Across it, he slid down to the stream to scoop water to slake his brittle thirst. It tasted of mud and rotten grass and leaves. He drank a little and worked it around his mouth and spit out its ugliness. Still, the water refreshed him and he took care not to drink too much and become sick.

Rising, he saw that the two buildings about fifty yards away were low frame structures, built about the same size, with head-high overhangs and enough roof pitch to keep snow from collecting. The unlighted building, he assumed, was the stable. The cabin had its door flung open with light from several lamps flooding out, the frame squeezing their glow into a bright rectangle, while a broken, irregular bar of yellow was painted on the rutted ground outside the door.

Away from the stream and the bridge, Ryerson melted into the darkness at the blind side of the cabin, his hands and arms poised, certain he was about to come face-to-face with Sam Cass and Lacey Bonner.

Still, he saw no horses in the yard and none in the primitive fenced corral beyond.

Light from the door was the only indication that people were in the place, or had been. Ryerson perceived no sound. Slowly he inched across the open space, ears pricked for any sound that would help identify the situation. He looked around in the dim moonlight for bodies or unusual activity.

Nearing the cabin, he stayed on the dark north side, moving up to hug it, measuring his breath. His ears searched for sound, but none came. He sensed that someone was inside. If it were Cass and Bonner, they were sleeping or he would hear something, loud talk, movement.

Sliding close to the low-slung shanty, Graydon's six-gun drawn, Ryerson rounded the corner in the dark and inched toward the doorway, feeling his way softly with his boot toes, putting his feet down only when he was sure of no telltale obstruction. A single window was perched head high, near the door, just under the roofline. It was heavily curtained inside with rough, thick material. A small band of light, invisible at a distance, crept under the curtain. Ryerson eased to it and peered inside with enough gap under the curtain to observe the big room.

A fireplace stood at the far end, flanked on one side by a small kitchen area with an open cupboard and a broad shelf for fixing food, and on the other side by a crude table. Taking up much of the cabin's floor space with its head against the far wall was a bed large enough for two people.

At the four corners of the bed, perched on a box, a small table, and at the foot end by a chair and another box, four glass-chimneyed lamps guttered as they poured soft light to fill the cabin and stream out the door—the bright yellow beacon he'd seen in the night.

Ryerson's attention centered in astonishment on the

bed. In the center of it a man was laid out in much the same way as Ryerson had left the body of Pat Graydon when he built his cairn. This man, however, was in his Sunday best—a worn and wrinkled suit of gray, his face the color of ashes and his bald head wreathed by close-cropped gray hair.

Peering through the narrow slit under the curtain, Ryerson also saw a large but young woman in the working dress of a ranch wife. Her long copper-colored hair, probably pinned up during the day, flowed luxuriantly over her shoulders and down her back. Ryerson turned away from the window and blinked; another redhead. His best friend, Dan Sturgis, killed in Civil War combat in Arkansas, and Ruby Montez, the all-too-brief second love of his life, drowned in one of his trouble-fraught law-keeping missions, were both redheads. Sometimes, the odd thought struck him, despite the urgency of the moment, that his life seemed filled with redheads.

Ryerson looked back into the room at the woman. She dozed in a vigil on a straight, slat-backed chair beside the body on the bed, a giant, double-barreled percussion shotgun resting across her knees and held firmly despite the fact that she dozed, her chin sagging on her chest.

In his quick appraisal, Ryerson surmised that the woman was much younger than the dead man, though probably not enough younger to be a daughter.

The reason for the open door on a cold night also became apparent; the heavy plank door had been beaten off its hinges and lay askew near the door frame on the hard-packed earthen floor.

His mind whirling, Ryerson stepped away from the window and dissolved into the dark the way he had come. Some thinking was called for. He could only surmise that Cass and Bonner had been here and were possibly responsible for the death of the man in the cabin. He didn't understand why the woman hadn't been ravaged as Stella Antrim had been. Maybe, he thought, grinning for the first time in a good many hours, her big-bore scattergun had something to do with it.

Near the rude bridge again, Ryerson stopped and looked back at the cabin bulking darkly against the night sky, accentuated by the shaft of yellow light playing out the vacant doorway.

He was well out of effective shotgun range, but within hailing distance. He looked at the sky and the narrow band of cold gray again oozing along the rolling eastern horizon. He suddenly felt very tired, knowing he had to muster the strength to look into the situation in the cabin. In another hour it would be light enough to see. He had slept but a few hours in two days and nights.

Taking a deep breath, Ryerson tensed himself, trembling a bit, shaking from the cold that had plagued him through the night. "Hello, the cabin!"

Even at the distance, his ears were keen on the scrape of a chair on the hard-packed earthen floor. There was no other sound. He visualized the woman coming abruptly alert and in fear, getting ready to defend herself and her home place.

"Hello, the cabin!" he called again. "I come as a friend. I mean no harm."

"Get on out of here if you know what's good for you!" came a hoarse cry from inside. The voice wavered as if from grief and fear and a host of other disturbed emotions.

"Please," Ryerson called back. "I'm here to help. I've been riding with Sheriff Graydon from Patchknife. I'm after two men who may have come this way. I represent the law."

"Come ahead then, but mind I've a loaded shotgun on you!"

"All right," Ryerson barked, moving toward the door. "Take it easy."

"Wait a minute! When you come through the door, have your hands high."

"Yes'm," Ryerson responded, continuing his slow walk from the bridge to the cabin, making no attempt now to be quiet. "Be careful," he said loudly, approaching the door. "Believe me, I come as a friend."

He raised his arms high as he stepped into the yellow rectangle of light on the ground. With another step he cautiously poked a foot inside, then stepped in. He stopped, hands still high. Slowly he allowed his gaze to sweep the room. Everything was as he had seen it in his quick glance through the window minutes before. The chair beside the dead man's funeral bed was now empty.

The woman stood at the back of the cabin in a seasoned stance, beside the fireplace and behind the table, holding the shotgun at her shoulder, head wedged against the butt stock and sighting down the barrels straight at him.

"State your business, mister!"

He made no abrupt moves. Though he could see her out of the corner of his eye, Ryerson stared straight ahead like a recruit being hazed by a superior officer. "I rode with Sheriff Graydon until yesterday afternoon when that pair bushwhacked and killed him. They're wanted for murder in Patchknife."

"Two big men with a string of horses they're trying to sell?"

"Aside from theirs, all those horses are stolen. May I put my hands down? It's been a long night. I've walked from where they killed Sheriff Graydon and stampeded our horses."

The woman eased her determined hold on the shotgun, still keeping it at the ready against her shoulder. "I know how to use this," she said.

"I don't care to test you," Ryerson said, dropping his arms. "Please believe me, ma'am. I mean no harm.

I'm badly in need of rest and something to eat and drink."

She inched from behind the table, lowering the shotgun, her distrust leaving her, but slowly. She'd still take some persuading. "They killed my man," she said flatly.

Ryerson's tension had also eased a bit. "I see."

"Leander was a good man," she said, as though it was a relief to tell someone. "For all that Leander was, he was a good man. Ah, I think you ought to take off your guns."

Ryerson looked at her, confused. "Those two men," he said. "Their names are Bonner and Cass. How long ago did they leave?"

"Hours ago. Before dark. They weren't here long. The guns, please."

"Doubtful they'd come back. But if it's all the same to you, I'd like to keep my guns on. For both our sakes."

She moved closer to him now, and he could see that despite her big frame and ample body, properly filled in the right places, she had rugged, substantial good looks crowned by full and long hair that was coppershiny as new telegraph wire.

Ryerson was reminded again of Ruby Montez, one of two women who'd had a deep significance in his life. It was a love he'd lost even before he could adequately express it; Cole Ryerson was not a man to plunge ahead heedlessly where women were concerned.

He caught her studying him closely, like a man, trying to take his measure as an adversary. Still she kept the shotgun at the ready, alongside her hip, but with the business end aimed at him. Her guard was only slightly relaxed; like me, she's been through a lot of suffering these last few hours, Ryerson thought.

Her eyes squinted at him. "No, take off your guns. If those two come back, I'll keep them away as I did yesterday evening. With this." She waved the shotgun barrels menacingly in a tight circle.

In no position to argue, Ryerson began untying, taking off and rolling up his gun rigs. "Have it your way," he said. He placed the bundles on her table, keeping the grips free. If he had to go for them, the guns wouldn't be all snarled in belts and tie-down thongs. The woman had moved away from him and edged closer to the bed. She still held the shotgun.

"Ma'am," Ryerson said, "I think Cass and Bonner are long gone. It'd help matters a great deal if you'd put that shotgun down. I, for one, don't want any accidents."

"Uh-uh. I figured you'd pretty quick get to trying to make me put down my gun. All the more reason to keep it handy. Why don't you sit in that chair by the bed, as far as you can get from those guns. First get yourself a drink with the dipper from that pail on the broad shelf."

The cold, rolled rim of the thin-metal dipper gave a pleasure all its own to Ryerson's parched lips. The water itself, ambrosia-like, offered sweet relief as it trickled down his throat. It was clear well water, and though it had been drawn many hours before, night chill had kept it fresh. He drank another dipperful before sitting in the chair while she edged past him cautiously to move toward her small kitchen.

"Sunup's breaking out there, and I'm used to fixing breakfast along about now. I was putting by my breakfast makin's for the two of us last evening when those horse merchants rode in. You can see there on the bed what they left me. Now, tell me a bit more about you and my good friend Sheriff Graydon. If your story's straight, I'll ask you to sit down and share my breakfast when it's ready. It's sure Leander won't be needing any. And no quick moves or you won't be needing any, either."

9

The body of Leander Folsom lay under a blanket, and the lamps had been blown out as bright sunlight filled the cabin. The Folsoms, as Kate Folsom told Ryerson, living so far out, were visited from time to time by the concerned Pat Graydon. Satisfied that Ryerson, too, had been Pat's trusted friend, Kate now sat easily across from him as they mowed away a stack of thick sourdough flapjacks, distinctively delicious, and light as the cumulus clouds Ryerson had seen near Patchknife two mornings before.

Kate Folsom appeared to be a bit rough-and-tumble, but not loose and lewd, like some frontier women he'd seen. She looked instead like one who could hold her own in almost any situation, with a sensitivity and tenderness about her that attracted Ryerson to her. She honestly grieved over the loss of her husband. Still, an attitude emerged in her that once a thing was done, it was past, and a person should begin remembering the good times and the mellow times and let go of the wasting emotion of grief as quickly as possible.

Hearing her speak this way, Ryerson realized he'd held on to his bitterness and anguish over losing Pat Graydon entirely too long. In those same feelings that

Kate expressed, there was no callousness nor lack of deep caring in her over Leander's death. She was hurting, but she was a woman of immense strengths to be able to handle it—another characteristic Ryerson felt he could benefit from.

Finishing her stack of flapjacks, Kate inched the chair back from the table, crossed her legs and cradled a large enameled cup of coffee in her hands like a hand warmer.

"You say their names were Cass and Bonner?"

"That's it. So Pat told me."

"They landed here a bit before dark. I was all for inviting them to get down and come in for supper until they took to getting mouthy with Leander out in the yard. Then I figured they could ride on and heat their own beans somewhere down the pike for all I cared."

"They were trying to sell the horses?"

"I stayed out there awhile listening to them jaw. But those two started to look at me in ways I didn't like, so I came on in the house and started fixing Leander's supper. I could hear them out there. They talked so loud I could make out what they said real plain, even with the door closed."

"What did your husband have to say?"

"Well, Leander wasn't talking so loud. But I've lived with the man ten years before and since we left Ohio, and believe me, you get to living with a person that long, you almost get to know what they're thinking. Surely you can understand even when they're talking low some ways off, like Leander was yesterday evenin'."

Kate paused, remembering. "They tried to get him to buy those extra four horses. Two of them had saddles, and I thought maybe they didn't belong to those two. It surely wasn't my place to say. But what man sells his horse and his saddle and all his personal gear unless the owner's dead? Or the horses were stolen with their saddles on?"

"The ones with saddles were mine and Pat Graydon's. Other two belonged to a couple of brothers named Antrim."

"The ones with the half-wit brother? You and Pat were riding with that pair and their foolish brother?"

"It's a long story. First tell me about Cass and Bonner."

"Well ... you know, Mr. Ryerson, I wonder if maybe Leander didn't recognize Pat's rig. It was a different horse than Pat rode down here before, but Leander was a smart man in his own way. If he'd seen that saddle and gear before, he'd remember."

"You think he might have said something to them about it that made them angry?"

"No. Leander was too smart for that. You say the horses belonged to the Antrim boys that live out east of Patchknife?"

"That's them."

"How'd you get tied up with the Antrims?"

"Well, Mrs. Folsom, it started when Cass and Bonner murdered Matt and Stella Antrim. The Antrim boys are out to hunt down Cass and Bonner and do them in on the spot. They threatened Pat Graydon and me if we got in the way. Pat and I sneaked into their camp while they were asleep and took their horses and their boots to buy us time to get Cass and Bonner ourselves and get them safely to jail in Patchknife to stand trial."

Kate Folsom cast an admiring eye on Cole Ryerson. "Aha! That must've taken some doing! I'd like to've been there. I've heard of Matt and Stella Antrim. Believe I saw her in Patchknife once. I really wouldn't know either of them from Adam's off ox."

"If he had one," Ryerson quipped, beginning to feel comfortable with the Folsom woman.

"Who?"

"Adam, father of us all. I didn't know he had an ox team."

"Oh," she said, chuckling. For the first time, Ryerson saw Kate Folsom smile. It was a good smile that probably would come easily under other circumstances.

Ryerson turned serious again. "Pat and I found where Bonner and Cass had camped and took a breather. The two of them had hung around, probably figuring we'd sniff out their camp, and set a trap to kill us. That's when they bushwhacked Pat."

"Such a fine man! And that's when they got all those horses?"

"We'd turned them out to graze. I was afoot, Pat was dead. Those two rode in easy and ran off with our mounts and two of the Antrims'. One horse got killed by mistake."

"Two of those saddle rigs had rifles in the stirrup boots. Leander probably smelled a rat about that, too. But I think he was too busy seeing a way to make some quick money."

"I piled rocks around Pat's body. Had no shovel. I've got to stop back that way sometime for a more thorough job. At least the varmints, the big ones, can't get to him."

"I'll go and help you," she said, as though there'd be no questioning her decision. Ryerson looked up at her from his food, started to say something and thought better of it. "Pat Graydon was a good friend," Kate continued. "He knew all about Leander's problem and tried to help what little he could."

Ryerson figured that at some point he'd learn more about Leander's "problem," so he let it ride. "That's when I started walking this way—after Cass and Bonner," he continued. "Sounds foolish, but it has to do with Pat and me being pardners years ago in New Mexico. He died on a mission, and I figured to see it through in his memory, or some such."

Kate Folsom's eyes again went wide in her astonishment. "Any other man would've turned back then and there. That's admirable, Mr. Ryerson, that's what it is. And you walked all the way here? My Lord, it must be twenty miles to the stage road alone up our lane. I don't know how far it is up to the country where you buried Pat. You came a far piece last night, I'll say that. No wonder you're having two flapjacks to my one!"

"Pat and I traveled light. Short rations."

"If you stayed around here, I'd see you properly fed."

Ryerson also chose to ignore that one. "Before that, we hadn't but jerky and beans and salt pork since leaving Patchknife. So I don't know if you're a good cook, Mrs. Folsom, but this breakfast is about the tastiest meal I can remember in a long, long time."

"I'm a good enough cook." Her self-assurance brought Ryerson's eyes up from his food. "That sourdough'll stick to your ribs, but won't lay heavy in the belly."

"I know. I've had my share of them, but nothing like these."

Kate Folsom was silent a long moment. "And here I am a widow lady, and not even thirty."

"Who was he? Leander, I mean."

She looked at Ryerson strangely. "He was my husband, of course. My man. Oh, he was a man of some means back home. That's how come I married him. He was fourteen years older. Our families had known one another and gone back and forth clear to my grandmaw's day. It seemed the most natural thing in the world that when I came of age, Leander came around to pay me court. All the women his age around there had been spoken for, so Leander stayed an old bachelor and saved his money."

"Your parents. They approved of that? Your marriage?"

"Oh, Daddy approved. There was nobody else in his mind. I tell you, Mr. Ryerson, Leander was a man of means. It's just that since we've been out here that he's slipped and it's all kind of gotten lost somehow."

"You came out from Ohio?"

"Monroe County. Five years ago. Two wagons and a hired man to drive one. That's how well-off Leander was. Took the steamer down the Ohio River to Sa'nt Louis, came out this way on the Santa Fe Trail. Loaded with his things and our china and fine furniture and some of my special things, but mostly new things we'd gotten for our home in a new land. But by and by we commenced to have trouble with the wagons, the animals coming up lame and the rain turning everything to gumbo and all, and Leander began throwing things out to lighten the load. I wished he hadn't done that. We could've gone slower. But he was changing, too. He went into violent rages if I as much as made a suggestion about things. So I let him have his way."

"Rough trails turn people that way sometimes," Ryerson said philosophically.

"Leander took sick a month to six weeks out of Sa'nt Louis. We were too far to turn back, and it was a long ways yet to go. While I was nursing him, the hired man took the other wagon and skedaddled. Headed back East. There wasn't a thing I could do, with a sick man in my wagon. Like Cass and Bonner, he took the team from our wagon with him, leaving Leander and me stranded."

"I guess you've had your problems, too, Kate."

"We waited there two weeks while Leander got better and before somebody came along that he could buy a team from. Leander had to pay ten times what they were worth. All our dreams were starting to wash away downstream. We came here and homesteaded this quarter section, and Leander figured to build a big cattle spread. What with bad winters and calves freezing in a late cold spell, poor market years and such and one thing after another, we've wound up with a few strays running around out there in the country. Leander didn't have enough money left nor enough cattle to pay to bring in hands, and the country's too big for him to ride alone. I'd've ridden with him, but first he wouldn't hear of it, and second, it still would've been too much even for the two of us."

Ryerson shook his head; it was a gesture of understanding.

"Then Leander started going off. He'd go to Medicine Springs or maybe into Patchknife, and be gone a week, two weeks at a time. I knew what he was doing. First his troubles got to him, and then the whiskey. It works that way on a man."

"Some men are like that," Ryerson said, not meaning it unkindly. He glanced at the body lying under the blanket, knowing the man that lay there had been cleaned and dressed and properly laid out by Kate's capable, loving and grieving hands. Then he thought of her being left alone in the hostile high plains in this cabin for weeks at a time. He found little respect for the lump of clay that was Leander Folsom.

"Oh," she said, her tone sounding like an apology for her late husband, "he'd come back full of regrets and new resolve. He'd be around a couple of days resting up, and I'd feed him good and get his strength back, and take good care of him. Then he'd get back to work. Oh, he'd work hard for a long time. Maybe as long as a couple of months, and I'd begin to have high hopes that things had begun to straighten out for us. All the time, I tried real hard not to fuss at him, and I took real good care of him so he wouldn't feel he had to run to town again."

"But he would," Ryerson said, feeling it was good for Kate to have someone to tell all this to.

"Oh, yeah." Kate was silent for a moment, thinking, reliving some of it. "We'd somehow get a few dollars ahead. I always needed things that he'd never bring back from town. He only took me along a couple of times, but that was pretty much before he started with the whiskey. I wouldn't pick at him because my daddy told me, if the preacher didn't, to love, honor, and obey. And never in my life, Cole, did I go against my father nor the teachings of the Bible. And never against my husband while he was alive."

"But Leander would go to town again." Ryerson felt it was important to encourage her.

Kate looked longingly at the blanketed body. "Sometimes we'd have extra vegetables or something to spare or he'd round up a steer or two that he could take in and sell and get our salt and flour and maybe a bolt of cloth for a new dress for me or something else we needed. And I'd try to tell him as gently as I could to get straight to town, do what needed to get done, and buy our things and turn around and head straight back. And he'd promise, faithfully. I believed him."

"And he'd be gone a week."

"Yeah," she said in a tired tone. "Sometimes more. He'd come back sheepish and empty-handed. So, I had more months to do without. Then I began to find his whiskey bottles hid in the stable. Or I'd find an empty bottle out in the roots of a tree in the field. That's where our money was going."

"What about Bonner and Cass, Kate? What happened last night?"

"They wanted Leander to buy those horses. He told them time and again he didn't have money to pay. They kept coming down on their price, insisting he must have some money somewhere. Finally he told them to let him take the horses to town and sell them, and he'd pay them top money. Told them to come back in a week. They said they couldn't wait that long. 'Course, I didn't know they were thieves and murderers. Then Leander tried to persuade them they could leave the horses and he'd pay them when they rode back through here next time. Or he'd send them the money. I could tell they were getting annoyed, and I knew what Leander was thinking, but it wasn't my place to come out of the cabin and say anything."

"Why'd they shoot him?"

"Those two pulled out a bottle and started passing it back and forth. Leander said if they were going to be partners in the horse-trading business, it was only right they let him have some. I could hear their voices getting louder and louder. Leander I guess made a grab for the bottle, and they flat-out shot and killed him dead."

"Then they came after you? That's when the door got knocked down?"

"The minute I knew Leander was shot, I bolted the door and grabbed my shotgun. I'd seen the way those two looked at me. I didn't want to use it on them, even though I knew they had killed my husband. I don't know why I didn't shoot into the door when they were beating it down, but I didn't. At first one of them pleaded with me to open it for them. He was the one that lorded it over the other. Bonner, I think it was."

"You're a lucky woman, Kate. They killed Mrs. Antrim after they both had their way with her."

Kate shuddered. "When I wouldn't let 'em in, they started beating on the door with stove wood from the yard, and in it came, like you see there. Hinges went before the hasp. When the door went down, I fired over their heads. You can see where I shot it there on the frame in the wood over the door. They were big men. Nigh filled the door frame."

Ryerson looked behind him to see an area over the door that looked as though the worms had been at it; peppered with holes of fine shot.

"I stood my ground, Cole, and told them that the next barrel would be theirs. They ran right back cursing something awful and got on their horses and vanished. In a while, when I got myself together and that, I went out and dragged Leander in and washed and dressed him in his good things and put him where you see him. Then I set the lamps like you saw when you came in, the way we did for dead folks back home, and I sat up with him the way a good wife should, but with my shotgun if those two came back."

"I suppose you'll want to bury him soon."

"It would be best. I'd be obliged for your help, Cole. I could do it, but—"

"I'll stay that long," Ryerson interrupted. "It's the least I can do. In return, do you have a horse I can use till I get mine back from Cass and Bonner?"

"There's a team in the barn. Draft horses, but when times were tough, I broke them to saddle. Leander's old saddle horse died."

"I know I'll come back this way with Cass and Bonner. I'll return your horse." He looked up to find Kate Folsom staring him straight in the eye.

"I'm going with you, Cole. I'm going to help you take the men that killed my husband and Pat Graydon back to Patchknife for their hangin'." Kate said it as though there would be no arguments.

10

The sun rode a noontime sky before Ryerson and Kate Folsom got Leander's body underground and his place for eternity properly marked with a piece of thick pine planking Ryerson found in the stable. With a spoke shave from the dead man's tools, Ryerson rounded the corners of one end of the marker to create something proper-looking in place of a headstone.

Kate had a good hand for lettering. While Ryerson toiled chopping a grave hole in the unyielding prairie sod on a rise a short way to the west of the ranch, she sat down to work with a small brush and black paint. Leander's marker proved to be an artistic job of putting down his name and age, and the date of his death along with a short, appropriate verse from the Scriptures.

Ryerson stopped briefly at his digging to let muscles loosen that ached for a rest. He squinted at the sun, thinking that for the second time in two days he was laying to rest a victim of Sam Cass and Lacey Bonner. The fire for justice in him when he left Pat Graydon's body had dwindled only slightly through his long night's ordeal. With the chore of building a proper resting place for Leander Folsom, it began to burn brightly again.

Kate carried her well-worn Bible when they went up to finish the burying and to secure the upright plank in the ground. He had faced the grave east so the marker would catch the morning sun and look toward the ranch as well as toward the eastern land Leander had come from.

Ryerson saw tears in Kate's eyes as she read her Bible passages over Leander's body. Now, as they walked slowly together down from the knoll back of the cabin, Ryerson toting the battered spade, her eyes were dry.

"I'm ready now to help you get those two that killed Leander," she said.

The thought of it had been on Ryerson's mind since she brought it up hours before. "Kate, pardon me, but I don't think that's such a good idea. Those men have already murdered four defenseless people. They'll be really desperate now. They won't hang any higher or be cut down deader if they killed me—and you—in the process."

Kate stopped and turned to him, the wind working in her long, coppery hair, anger flashing in her eyes. "Mr. Ryerson! I have no notion of dying! From what you said, Mr. and Mrs. Antrim were caught unawares and beat up pretty bad before they were killed. And Pat Graydon didn't have a chance, either. As for Leander, well, he'd become a foolish man, and I'd known it for a long time. The day he died, he did some of the most foolish things ever."

"But—"

Kate interrupted quickly. "No buts. I'm a strong woman, Mr. Ryerson. If you don't think I can get by on this land, well, sir, you just try living out here— alone much of the time—for five or six years. I've had to run off wolves and kill snakes. I've chopped and fetched my firewood, and lots of times I've had to make do with nothing to keep body and soul together when he was off on one of his drunks in town. I'm a strong woman and proud, Mr. Ryerson. When those two came through that door last evenin', don't you think they didn't know where I stood! I'm a firm believer that 'Thou Shalt Not Kill.' But I would have if they hadn't git when they did. And I can thrash a man if need be. Many's the time it crossed my mind to show Leander a thing or two for his foolish ways that were tearing me apart inside, but it wasn't my place."

Ryerson, taken by surprise at her outburst, decided against saying anything for the moment, but started for the cabin.

"You need rest, Mr. Ryerson," she said, her long skirt rustling in the grass as she strode to catch up with him. "You go in the cabin and crawl up on the bed and get some sleep. I'll see to pulling things together that we'll need, and some food. When we travel, you won't be eating jerky and beans, I'm here to tell you. You'll eat decent food, properly fixed."

Ryerson glanced over his shoulder as the big-boned woman with the pile of gleaming russet hair came up to him. She was very determined and, as she said, was as proud as she was strong. "All right," he said, knowing when to pull away from an argument. It was certain this woman was no shrinking violet. "Do you know the country to the south? That's where we'll head. They've traveled south straight as a string since leaving Patchknife. The moon will still be in full phase. If I get a little sleep now, we may be able to ride most of the night. Maybe catch them first thing in the morning."

Kate flounced easily alongside him, much in control of herself and hardly acting like the bereaved widow. "Once, when Leander was away," she said, "and we still had a milch cow, I had to track her down that way when she got out. She was gone most of the night, so I spent all day hunting her up and was down in that country. Saw some good spots for camps that way. More than that I don't know."

Ryerson held back to let Kate enter the cabin. He stopped to examine the door frame where the hinges had been ripped free by the battering of Cass and Bonner. "After a while I think I can take a few minutes to peg those screw holes for the hinges and rehang the door. That way we won't have to leave the welcome mat out for the varmints while we're gone." He realized he was already speaking of the two of them as a team.

"For all manner of varmints," she said. "Even the two-legged kind. You must be right handy with tools. I'll be much obliged."

The bed had a welcome look. The calves of his legs ached from his walking and lack of rest and from digging Leander Folsom's grave and burying him. His brain was foggy with fatigue as well, and he knew a few hours' rest would refresh and sharpen him.

Although he should have felt uncomfortable about going to sleep in a strange woman's home—a recent widow at that—it had come down to that, and that's all there was to it. He sat on the edge of the soft mattress that beckoned him to stretch out and sleep. He pulled off his boots and lay back, feeling a depression where Leander's body had been. He propped his head on a pillow and thought, so what? Life is for the living.

It was cool in the cabin's dim twilight despite the clear, warm afternoon. Kate appeared beside him holding a comforter, which she spread over him. "Now harken well, Cole Ryerson. I haven't had much sleep, either. When I get things ready for us when we ride, and see what we've got for supper, I'm figuring to crawl up there beside you. Now you needn't fret about a thing or think me forward. No man lays a hand on me less'n I want him to. There is no reason in God's green earth that the two of us shouldn't have some good bed rest before we start out."

As she spoke, standing over him, Ryerson watched her from the pillow, his eyes squinted. His first impulse was to jump up, demand a horse and ride on alone, right now. If he did ride, he'd have to do it on less than the short rations he'd had with Graydon. He needed the rest, the food she'd fix to take along, the blankets, and the warm coat by the door, which was no longer needed to warm the frame of Leander Folsom. Ryerson realized he was giving up, making compromises with himself, vulnerable because he was exhausted.

Again he sighed. "We do what we have to do, Mrs. Folsom." Ryerson closed his eyes.

"Sleep well, Mr. Ryerson," she said, responding to his formality.

The sun was low behind the cabin when Ryerson awoke. Already the yard lay in the long shadow of the building, and daylight seeped out of the large, single room. The bed was narrow, and Kate Folsom lay curled up, facing him, a peaceful, almost girlish expression on her sleeping face. Ryerson studied the widow's reposed face, his respect for her growing. She slept outside the thick quilt covering him. Cautiously, he edged off the other side of the bed from under the cover and slid his socked feet quietly to the floor.

Around the cabin the land lay peaceful and serene at the end of the day. In the dim twilight as he tiptoed around for his boots, he saw that the table beside the fireplace was piled with the necessities of travel. Leander's heavy trail coat had been tossed on top of two rolls of blankets, expertly tied and ready to be secured behind saddles. Two pairs of saddlebags bulged with food and other necessities for the trip. From one jutted the black handle of a small, cast-iron spider for frying.

Several boxes of rifle ammunition and her powder flask, shot pouch, and other essentials for the shotgun lay on the table, while against the wall, next to her shotgun, leaned a businesslike and new-looking Winchester lever-action. In a quick glance, he saw it was chambered for .44 cartridges, as was Graydon's six-gun. She hadn't forgotten a thing.

As Ryerson tiptoed around, checking out the things she had prepared, he mused that there could be worse things than having her along. The essentials were laid out for a good trip, with nothing forgotten and nothing useless tossed in—and, he had begun to enjoy Kate Folsom's company.

As he started for the door with the bedrolls to search out and saddle the horses, she woke, rolled on her back and stretched languidly to shrug off sleep, and sat up.

"Howdy," he said from the doorway. "Feeling better?"

"Great improvement," she said. "How about you?"

"That was what I needed. Guess I can go after them now. It'll be full dark soon. I figured to go look to what you have for saddle gear for the horses while there was still light, get them saddled up and loaded and brought up to the house. It'll take me ten minutes or so after that to fix the door."

She still looked at him from the bed. "You're a good man, Cole Ryerson. And a gentleman. That's pretty rare around here and in these days. I knew that before I had any thoughts of bedding down here beside you."

"Well, I thank you for that," he said. "I'll look to the horses."

"While you're getting things tied up, I'll fix us some supper. I've got some cured ham and a mess of hen's eggs in a cold crock. There's a couple of loaves of good sourdough bread in the things I put by there, but I saved half a loaf for our supper. From the looks of you, I'd say you're good for a couple thick ham slices warmed, and about six of those eggs and a few slices of bread spread with my preserves."

"That'll about fill the bill," Ryerson said, his stomach grumbling agreeably at her suggestions. He watched as Kate slid to the edge of the bed and sat a moment looking around.

"I'd better light a lamp or two," she said, getting up. "You know, Cole, Leander was a foolish man, or got to be that way. There wasn't much left between us. But it's going to do my heart good to ride down there with you and get a rope around that pair and haul them back to Patchknife. And I aim to stick around for the hanging."

Ryerson nodded and turned to head for the barn. By the time he got the horses saddled and bridled and had tied on the bedrolls and brought the animals up to the house, it was dark. Light from Kate's lamps again oozed through the vacant door frame and spread its soft, long beam on the ground.

The cabin filled with the tantalizing smells of warmed ham and frying eggs and of sourdough bread being warmed. Ryerson found some tools to help with the job and began whittling pegs to fill the holes where the hinge screws had stripped loose.

Kate had changed from her dress into clothing for the trail; a pair of Levi's jeans that had probably been Leander's conformed to every curve of her strong and ample hips and thighs. Above her tight waist, a faded blue work shirt flared provocatively around large, firm breasts. Kate had rolled the sleeves a turn or two, and Ryerson saw solid, tanned arms and strong, capable wrists. There was, he mused, nothing weak or prissy about the woman.

She had pulled her hair up and pinned it, hiding most of it under a tan slouch hat. Strands of the soft, copper-colored hair still managed to sneak loose around her ears and the nape of her man-sized neck.

Suddenly Ryerson was not in the least displeased that he'd have her as a companion on the trail. Already he was working on ways to use her presence to nab Cass and Bonner without putting her welfare on the line. An idea for a trap, a way to get them off guard, had hatched in his head.

"Could you fix that door after supper, Cole?" she asked. "Everything's ready."

"Well, I reckon," he enthused. "First things first."

"Then come over here and belly-up to my table!"

11

The land stretched before them without end.

Ryerson and Kate Folsom had ridden all night, keeping the bulking silhouettes of the mountains against a star-studded sky to their right, moving ever southward. They talked little while riding, chatting only when they stopped to give the horses a rest and to stretch legs and hips that over the hours had tightened and cramped from straddling the wide backs of the workhorses. But there was an everlasting, untiring rhythm to their gait.

Rain, a common occurrence in this land, held off. As it had for several days that Ryerson had been on the trail, dawn seeped in with a gray tint out of the land to the east, a band that grew wider and gradually bluer as the sun pushed the night ahead of it. Clouds had moved in overhead and to the east of the riders; the dawning sky painted the clouds with the rose and pink magnificence of a high plains sunrise.

The man and woman riding south and buried within the folds of an enormous land marveled at the awesome depth of color as they drank in its beauty. They breakfasted lightly, and by midday came on a wide and shallow river, fringed by trees. Through irregular breaks in the trees on the south bank, Ryerson could see that beyond the river the land quickly resumed its easy, rolling, grassy character, which by now had an almost monotonous quality.

The river, flowing lazily and thin over sand and gravel bars, carried scarcely a ripple and appeared to pursue a nearly true course from west to east, flowing down from the mountains. Because of its languid movement and the general flatness of the land it cut through, the river had no need to buck and curve, but lay straight as a stretched rope, wearing its fringe of trees like a lace border.

The air was cooler under the trees than out in the glaring mid-morning sun that had warmed them as they rode. "Pleasant spot," Ryerson remarked.

"Let me fix us a good meal here, Cole," she said. "Must be we've been in the saddle the most part of sixteen hours."

"The horses need a rest," he said, "as if we don't." The spiritless but solid horses stood unattended by the water's edge and drank. Hardly spooky, they would need no hobbles during their rest, but would probably wander into the grass near the line of trees at the bank and graze like cattle, contented in the sun. Ryerson watched them, remembering that the last time he had let horses graze free, it ended in disaster. He didn't think Cass and Bonner would try the same stunt twice, but he remained on the alert, keeping Leander's Winchester close at hand. They'd seen no evidence of the outlaw pair since sunrise enabled them to see clearly.

Kate studied the sluggish stream whose water was only slightly muddy from moving dirt washed from its banks. It had hardly the clarity of a mountain stream, but one could still see into its shallow depth. The stream bed appeared to be deepest close to the banks, while at midstream it was humped with gravel and some boulders and small stones. The only ripples were in the middle, as water broke over or flowed around obstacles close to the surface.

"I'll bet there's some good holes in there along the bank," she said. "I could use a bath. Couldn't you? There's a little jar of soft soap in my things, and I brought along some towels."

"You thought of everything," he said.

"Cole, why don't you go off up there and go bathing while I get our meal." She went to the horses, rummaged in the saddlebags and found the soap and a towel for him. She also fished out the food she meant to fix.

"Want me to build a fire?" he asked, standing by the stream and watching it, feeling its presence begin to relax the tension of his long hours in the saddle.

"You men!" Kate said. "Do you think I can't build a decent cookfire for myself? Get along with you, Mr. Ryerson. Here!" She tossed the soap jar and towel at him. He grabbed for the soap, which sailed at him fast, while the towel floated away short of his reach.

"Well, if you ain't Mr. Butterfingers," Kate said, laughing, a relaxed tone in her voice and in her laugh. He liked that. The trip, despite its dangers, was probably good for her, better indeed than being left alone in that cabin with the fresh grave staring down from the knoll. He, too, was glad for her company. He felt himself brightening inside, if only because she was with him.

He was aware that a closeness had developed out of their common purpose.

Now he only looked at her, picked up the towel, slung it over his shoulder and headed upstream toward a likely looking spot for a dip. A short distance away, trees with the lush foliage of summer leaned over the river, shielding him from the crossing. A massive boulder lay beyond and off the bank, forming a dam the water had to swirl around. The river, in working its way past the obstacle, had chewed a deep, man-sized basin upstream of the rock, showing him a clear three- or four-foot depth, and long enough for a man to stretch out in. The water here was clear and clean.

Ryerson stroked a four-day growth of dark bristle on his chin that probably did a good job of disguising him. His razor, brush, and mug were in his saddlebags on a horse being led in the string by Bonner and Cass. For now, he'd have to forego the luxury of a shave. For all her thinking ahead, Kate probably didn't stick in Leander's razor and strop. Besides, he thought, it would be better to look unshaven and tough when he encountered the killers.

He looked downstream, assured that no one was in sight. He pulled off his boots and skinned out of his clothing for the first time in days. He felt a freedom in his nudity, the cleansing feeling of the air and its breezes on every part of him, a primal sensation—a throwback, he often thought, to a time when people went around most of the time without much by way of covering. Even without getting into the water, he already felt renewed.

Crouching, he slid to the water's edge and tested it with a toe. The water had come down from the mountains and, ever-shielded from the warm sun by overhanging trees, was still crisply cold. He sat on the bank and stretched in his legs to the knees, feeling the chill of it setting his muscles a-tremble. He slid off the bank into the water's iciness, abruptly immersing himself to above the waist, bringing a choked gasp in spite of himself. The major shock of it grabbed his genitals in a frigid fist. For a long time he stood there, hugging himself against the cold, waiting while his lower half accepted the chill, feeling it already flooding him with vigor.

With much of his body tolerating the water's biting contrast to the balmy air, Ryerson took a deep breath and jumped with a great splash, throwing his legs ahead of him and dropping beneath the surface on his butt, bearing his lightened weight on his hands and arms, and coming up gasping and blowing. He grabbed for the soap jar, waded out of the hole and lathered himself from top to bottom. Tossing the jar back on the bank, he crouched and made a short head-first plunge into the hole, reaching out with his arms for protection from the big rock and slithering to the bottom while the soap was quickly rinsed from his skin. Now the keen bite of the water was enjoyable.

On the bank, he slapped and stroked off most of the water before drying himself briskly with the coarse towel, feeling it work wonders to invigorate his frigid skin. He tingled while he dressed as blood again found its way to the surface of his skin, radiating the euphoria of being clean. He felt brighter and more optimistic than he had since Graydon's death. He worked his hat down over his damp hair, combed back with his fingers, grabbed the soap jar, tossed the towel over his shoulder and strode jauntily back to the crossing where Kate busied herself getting their meal.

She had baked a potato for each of them in mud balls jammed close to the embers of her fire. Two thick slabs of sourdough bread spread with berry preserves and well-warmed ham waited for him on an enameled plate. "This is what I call choppin' in pretty tall cotton," he said, moving toward the colorful, beckoning plate.

"I told you I know how to take care of a man," Kate said. "If you need a drink, I guess you can dip a cupful from the river. I'll make coffee when we stop tonight. I was a little low on coffee before we left, so we've got to stretch it."

Ryerson attacked the food like a man with a supreme hunger, squatting close to her and the fire. His dip in the icy water and the glow of being clean had honed his appetite to a fine edge. This meal was almost finer than the sourdough flapjacks the morning before.

"Well, you sure look better," she continued, breaking open a mud ball and cleaning a potato for him. "Not that there was much a body could find fault with before that. Good spot to swim up there, Cole?"

"Cold," he responded, ignoring her first remark. "Colder than hell."

"Why do they say 'colder than hell'? Hell's supposed to be hot."

"Meaningless. Why did Bonner and Cass kill four innocent people? I don't know, Kate. Another of those pointless things."

A cloud crossed her expression. "You had to bring that up, did you? I was starting to relax and enjoy this place and being with you and beginning to forget the awful things of the past couple of days." Her voice had taken an edge.

"I'm sorry," he said. "Sorry I brought it up. It was on my mind, I guess."

"Aw, Cole, I didn't mean to snap at you."

"I didn't see it as a snap, Kate. You've been through a lot."

"A woman doesn't lose a husband every day. Things suddenly change. Suddenly I've changed." She was quite a direct woman, Ryerson thought; little beating around the bush. "There never was love, really. With Leander. There was affection. Caring. Maybe it was one-sided, but it was there. For a while. The last four or five years weren't exactly a honeymoon."

"I understand," Ryerson said, like her, not wanting to be reminded of the evil of the past few days. "When you want to bathe, go past those two big trees about to topple in. A big rock. Above it is a good spot. But try the water with one foot first. You may change your mind. I almost did. And the surface chill is nothing. The deeper you go, the colder it gets."

"You went in, didn't you? You had your bath."

"It took some doing."

"Well, then don't worry about me, Mr. Ryerson. I told you. I'm a strong woman."

"And human. That water's cold. You don't have to answer to me."

Something in her manner said she was trying to prove herself to him. Leander Folsom probably rarely took notice of her strengths of character.

She got up. "Get some rest," she said. "I'll be back in a few minutes and pack things." Kate grabbed the soap jar and a dry towel and wandered away. Ryerson used the last of a hunk of his bread to sop up some tasty ham juice on his plate.

Watching Kate disappear upriver, he wandered to the water's edge and with some wet sand scoured his enameled plate, rinsed it and waved it to dry before wandering back to put it among her things.

In the quiet, peaceful setting, the river slithering a few feet away, a soft, comfortable, lazy feeling came over Ryerson. For a time the hazardous mission could be set aside. He stretched out in a soft, grassy spot where the sun broke through the overhead leaves. The grass was dry, and the earth, warmed by the sun, sent a good feeling into his body, only a little stiff from his hours in the saddle. His head found a mound for a soft pillow. He propped his hat over his eyes and closed them. He folded his hands on his chest and quickly drifted into a soft, tentative kind of slumber.

His consciousness was aroused, not knowing how long he had slept, by her whispered voice. "Cole?" It had a throaty, lulling quality, and he did not move, keeping the shield of his hat over his face. He sensed her close to him. The sun was warmer now in the spot where he'd napped.

Kate drew herself to him intimately; within himself, he found no reason to resist or draw away.

An arm felt its way across his chest lightly and lovingly. He grunted in response.

"It's hard to get hold of in my mind," she whispered, her lips close to his ear. He lay relaxed, still without shying away, knowing what was happening and accepting it. Sometimes, he reasoned, it was best not to ask questions for which there were no answers. He found himself enjoying what was happening, aware of his own long-bottled-up need, knowing he was willing to flow with the tide of the moment.

"I'm free, Cole. No longer bound by vows." Her hushed tone was not meant to be persuasive. It was a flat statement, but one of near delight. "Ten years can be a lifetime. Leander Folsom was aged beyond his years, dry and lifeless as an old leaf. I know how good it can be. I had friends at home who married men nearer their years. I am sorry, truly sorry for him now that he's dead. But I'm free now. Free! Is it wrong to be in need, now that I'm free?"

Ryerson didn't answer, and that in itself was a positive response.

Her hand, which had rested on his chest, came up and lifted the hat to see if he was listening. He felt the sun in his eyes through the lids, but kept them closed. "I'm here," he said. He could feel and smell her sweet, warm breath on his face, and knew without looking that she was bent over him. He felt the long, damp, clean-smelling hair flow over his face, shivering against its caress as it tickled his ears and the skin not covered by bristles. Her lips brushed his gently, but with a hunger radiating in their warmth.

The yearning rose up in him slowly but steadily, mounting in its intensity. Their lips joined with passion, probing with mutual need. Against his, her lips were soft, full, moist, warm and yielding, filling him with a desire that roared through his system like a raging fire, welling up like a broad river at flood.

Groping to meet her embrace, he slid an arm around her, reaching for her side, her back. She had not buttoned the shirt after her swim, and his palm slid over still-damp skin soft as lush winter fur.

She broke from their passioned embrace and kiss to mutter an exclaimed "Ohmahgod!" and then was silent. Ryerson opened his eyes to find her so close he could see the flecks of color as well as the delight in her green eyes, and the free-flowing strands of hair stuck together by dampness and curling past her temple. Her features this close to him were soft, smooth and unlined. She smiled—a smile of pleasure and abandonment to the moment. A smile of love and of giving.

Ryerson shut his eyes as hers did, and she again directed her lips at his for the soaring thrill of contact.

"I have a great need," she hissed, gasping as her mouth found his. "Such a great need!"

12

Their brief but warm interlude at the river with its momentary forgetting was the key that turned the manhunt in their favor. They had been back on the trail hardly an hour when Ryerson found a stack of greenish-brown horse turds and believed he could see vapor rising from them. Even from horseback, his nostrils were keen on their acrid smell.

His insides leaped with encouragement; while he had caught only catnaps, Cass and Bonner, convinced they were virtually home free, were getting their full nights' sleep and dawdling on the trail. The grass was sufficiently broken and bent to assure him that the two still led four stolen horses. Despite these signs, caution was called for.

"We've got to go slow from here," he told Kate. "I don't want them setting a trap for us the way they did for Graydon and me. What they did once, they could do again."

Three times, as they approached large rises in the rolling grassland, Ryerson got down and scouted the land ahead on foot, sneaking up the blind side of the knolls, eyes probing ahead for sign of the killers and their telltale remuda. The small horse herd also tended to slow the outlaws' flight, he reasoned.

Ryerson's third scout was the charm. He slid back off the hill and loped back through the tall grass to her. Kate sat her horse, holding the reins of his. "They're out there, aren't they, Cole? I can tell."

"A grove," he said. "About two miles out. The horses are bunched, grazing." He looked at the sky, calculating how much was left of the day. "Are you ready to take them?"

"In this, Cole? They'd see us coming the minute we came over that rise. Surely we can't ride out into open country at them in broad daylight!"

"No, Kate. Nothing like that. They're going to find us. I've worked on this one since we left your place. Uh-uh. They'll find us!"

"What?!"

"The timing is perfect. It couldn't have worked better. We'll swing east, from the looks of the land. It's lower out there. We'll be well-screened. Then south. Below them. They're probably settling in for the night. I saw smoke from their fire. That's why we've come on them so quickly. They haven't traveled fast. Right now, since they killed Graydon and put me afoot, they don't think the law is too close behind. They've no notion of the Antrims being on their trail, so they think they're free of them, too. They're riding under a false sense of security."

"But ride by them? Then what? Lay in wait?"

Ryerson hooked a toe in his stirrup and pumped himself into the saddle of the tall draft horse. "Exactly. We'll ride east. Get ahead of them as far as we can tonight. Come on."

He swung his horse to their left, following the screen of rolling hills, and headed for the protection of another to make a wide sweep well out of sight of Cass and Bonner.

"All right, Mr. Ryerson," Kate called, spurring to

join him. "Don't keep me waiting. Give me the rest of it."

"We'll come back in south of them, and I'm afraid, my dear, that we'll have to go into a dark camp just in case. But come sunup, I'll build a hell of a smoky fire to lure them in."

"Is that wise?"

"They really only know you, Kate. I was hidden in the grove when Pat was shot. They only saw me riding in at a distance. I was still in the trees when they ran off the horses. They'll never expect me to be camping south of them. Men who operate as directly as they do won't think in terms of someone dealing indirectly with them. They're looking back over their shoulders for pursuit, not ahead. As far as they know, I'm still on foot. Probably they think I headed back for Patchknife for help. All that's what'll have them off guard in the morning."

"What about me? They both had a good look at me."

"They won't see you. At first. If it's early enough, you'll be rolled in your blankets. All I tell them is that you're my pard, still asleep. If they come by much later, you'll still be my pard, sleeping off too much John Barleycorn. We'll give it every element of surprise. If they think we might have whiskey—I imagine they're getting dry now—they'll have that in their minds, another factor in our favor."

"You can't take them alone, Cole. It's too risky."

Ryerson reined his horse around and came up alongside her. He leaned off his horse to kiss her, brushing his lips against the velvet softness of hers. "That's where you come in, Mrs. Folsom, if you're as strong as you say you are. Under the blanket, you'll have the shotgun cocked. We'll have some code word, and when I say it, you swing up the shotgun from under the blankets and we'll have them dead to rights. They won't dare make a move with my two sidearms and both barrels of that howitzer of yours trained on them. I know. I've already had the experience of looking down those muzzles!"

"I'm scared, Cole."

"No, not scared. You're anticipating being scared. Hell, lady, you've already faced them down once and run them off with their coattails flying. You were scared then, but you didn't let it get in the way. I daresay they've a healthy respect for those two barrels of death of yours, and the look of you when you've got blood in your eye. They've got plenty to be scared of from us, that's what! Remember that. I could sneak into their camp tonight and take them off guard. But I'd rather handle it the other way. Otherwise, we're both dead tired when we take them, and that's more of a risk." He reefed on the reins to ride on.

"Either way it's risky, isn't it?" she called after him.

"They'll be more off guard riding into the camp of a couple of saddle bums south of them in the morning. Probably they'll figure when they ride in, to rob us and kill us. When we surprise them and come up alert and mean business, the shoe'll be on the other foot."

"You think we can pull it off, Cole?"

"I wouldn't try it if I didn't. Was your hair down when they were in your yard the other day?"

"Yes. Why?"

"Leave it down when you're covered in the blanket in the morning. When you come rolling out of there with your shotgun armed and ready and they see that hair, it'll take 'em a few seconds to get things sorted out in their heads. It'll give us the edge we need."

By the start of the prairie's long twilight, Ryerson had found a spot for them to camp and bait their trap for Cass and Bonner. After riding south for more than an hour, Ryerson felt they were well below the fugitives. They turned west again to find a place the murderers and their string of horses would surely pass by.

After the many twists and turns of his ordeal, it was

almost too natural, too easy. The land north of Ryerson and Kate sloped down easily to a broad, gentle coulee that spread for miles. The terrain, he thought, would incline the two to take the path of least resistance and the bed of this low south-bearing depression in the land.

He calculated that Cass and Bonner would be almost due north of their position. In the morning, the outlaws would be on a collision course with his and Kate's camp. A tributary draw with a trickle of water merged with the larger cleft in the land. Trees grew here, providing an excellent campsite for shade and firewood at the edge of the ditchlike brook.

While Kate readied the place for the night and set about pulling together another meal, Ryerson made a short scout to the north. If Cass and Bonner had stayed put, Kate could risk a cooking fire.

His pulse quickened with the thought that he and Kate would again share their blankets and their mutual warmth this night. Riding back from his reconnoiter, he thought again about the only two other women who had meant anything in his life. Ruth Bascom Sturgis was herself a widow two years, after the wartime death of her husband and Ryerson's best friend, when she turned down Ryerson's offer of marriage. His mind's eye replayed the tragic death of Ruby Montez in a raging river; his feelings toward Ruby, though brief, had the depth of sincerity. Now he had begun to care about a woman again. She'd been widowed such a short time that his feelings were hard to understand. But they were good and honest feelings, and there was nothing, really, wrong about having them.

In other times and other places, he knew, what had happened between them would be frowned upon. A woman observed a respectable time of chastity and solitary grief in black clothing, hiding her face behind the cloaking veils of sorrow and grief.

But this, he mused, was the West and the high

plains, and this was a manhunt; traditional conventions were somehow out of place and needed to be set aside. Leander Folsom had been a great deal less than a fitting husband, lover, and provider for that woman back there now bustling about pulling together a good evening meal for the two of them. In these perilous times and these risky places, he thought, life had to go on; civilized convention and tradition must be set aside.

Besides, Ryerson thought, if there were any slipups, all this could be over with the suddenness of a pistol shot anyway. So, he reasoned, rather crudely—but it was an honest thought—to hell with Leander Folsom. To hell with musty conventions about widowhood. Her man was gone. That was over. She said so herself. Right now Kate Folsom needed Cole Ryerson. And Lord knows, he thought, I need her! I need her strength and her tenderness. Those notions stayed with him a long moment. He half smiled into the gathering darkness. A strange glow—best classified, he thought, as deep affection, maybe lust—worked its way inside his chest. Damn, he thought warmly, Kate Folsom was some woman, a combination of the best he'd found in Ruth Sturgis and Ruby Montez. And Kate, after years of a devoted but barren marriage to Leander Folsom, needed him.

He mused on it riding back to her as dusk slid from gray to a darkness that would soon verge into deep night. The night would turn cold anywhere, and colder here where they were camped by a stream.

Just now, the day's long journey into twilight brought a balmy, heady fragrance to the land; hard to define. Prairie fragrance. Perhaps, he thought, smiling at his own innocence and naiveté, it was all in his head. A head full of sugarplum visions and the hot nuts of manhood. The night with Kate at the camp was something to anticipate. Again his mind dwelled on a slipup in the morning. This night could be an end—or a beginning. It was certain to be the end of intimacy. With the hoped-for capture of Bonner and Cass, their growing familiarity would be changed, if not totally over. Temporarily, at least.

At this point in his life, heaven only knew what the hours and the days—even the weeks—would bring. He projected it in his thoughts; always good to have a plan, he mused. With the killers in tow, who knew what kind of challenges all that would bring? It was for sure that Kate would weather it. Despite a gentle femininity that she'd shown him in many ways, there was an almost masculine toughness in her. He smiled again; she'd do okay. He thought about her, building a comforting possessiveness; Cole Ryerson's kind of woman.

Letting his horse set its own pace through the gloaming, Ryerson sensed that it was good to think of the here and now, and of the woman waiting for him over the next ridge, busying herself in his absence with his needs, bustling around with the camp comforts and working up a meal a man would delight in wrapping himself around.

Little was to be feared now. In his scout, he had seen no sign of Cass and Bonner in this part of the country. He was certain they were holed up miles to the north. If his plan worked, he'd take them in the morning and be headed for Patchknife. The only true dark cloud on the horizon was a possible confrontation with the Antrims.

With Pat Graydon, he might bull that one through; under current conditions, Kate Folsom was a questionable quotient.

That was a coming threat, too, he'd have to deal with. By now the brothers had found some means of getting somewhere in their stockinged feet, and found horses and footgear, even if they had to badger some poor hand-to-mouth cuss like Leander Folsom for them. Back went his thoughts to Kate Folsom and her widowhood. The times, he thought, were a-changing. Old customs, like the time of mourning in widowhood, and the old values, had fallen all along the line. Likewise, the Indian's way of life was going, the pride and fierce independence withering and crumbling under the influence of the white man's greed and whiskey, disintegrating like the dead leaves of fall.

The white man's way, too, Ryerson thought, letting the big workhorse set its own pace, was undergoing change. The war had brought a lot of it to pass, ushering in a new mood of greed and a special brand of evil riding on the tide of eastern migration moving ever westward, into every corner of the land.

It came, Ryerson thought, under the heading of progress. For every victory, it stood to reason, there had to be a defeat. Somewhere, somebody lost. Kate losing the need of the sackcloth-and-ashes cloak of widowhood. And, sadly or gladly, it worked in his favor.

As he topped a rise under pleasant but fading light to look down at the campsite, and seeing through the graying distance the woman happily at her chores, he thought, maybe I've joined them without knowing it. Maybe I'm as evil and greedy and viciously self-serving as the bastards I loathe—Bonner and Cass and the Antrim boys. He grunted again at the depth of his thoughts, and spurred his horse down the slope to where Kate Folsom's cooking fire twinkled a welcome through the looming darkness.

His mind turned on the comforting lights of home for a man coming back to them. He wanted and needed that and would have it. He would contest Cass and Bonner and the Antrim brothers for his right. He would fight and conquer for that! For Kate and a home!

13

Dawn broke as dawns had broken for several days since Ryerson had started on the killers' trail. The sun bulged with fiery magnificence off the eastern horizon, its light prying under Ryerson's eyelids, waking him. He blinked against it, and then with eyes closed, groped for his hat and covered his face, reluctant to break the bond with sleep.

This morning differed from the others in a very special way. Kate Folsom was curled beside him, close enough to touch. The warmth of her body radiated into his, the dawning sun not disturbing her deep sleep.

Ryerson eased an arm out of the blankets, lifted the hat and, holding it up, studied her. Her face was turned toward him, as angelic and serene in sleep as it had been that late afternoon in her cabin before they left to continue the manhunt. Her hair was down, and hadn't been rumpled much by the night. As the gray light seeped away to be replaced by the bright sun, it glinted off her coppery hair, tinting it with fire. Her hair still glowed from its washing at yesterday's river. Ryerson acknowledged he had a weakness for redheads. He had a notion to stroke her hair, but it was too soon to wake her. Or was it?

With a dart of alarm, he remembered that they were here to trap Cass and Bonner. If the pair had started out with the first glimmerings of dawn, they could ride over the far knoll at any moment.

He stroked her hair anyway, to waken her gently. "Katie?"

"Hah-dee," she said, her voice soft and sweet, reflecting the waking-up contentment with what had taken place between them in the moments after rolling up in their warm soogans.

"It's damned early, but we'd better get ready. No telling when the guests will arrive."

Realization brought her abruptly alert. She missed his joke. "Okay. Is there time to fix something to eat?"

"You'd better stay wrapped up, Kate. Maybe make a quick trip into the bushes. There's still some of last night's coffee in the pot by the fire. It may be a bit strong, but it'll be hot. The coals are still glowing."

"We've got to have something, Cole."

Just like a woman, he thought. "I'll spread some of the bread with preserves and heat some beans. That'll have to do, Kate. Beans'll heat fast when I kick up the fire."

Ryerson climbed out of the blankets when she did, shrugged into Folsom's worn trail coat and pulled the collar up, as much to hide his face as to keep his neck warm in these chill moments before the sun warmed the land. The coat was cold, but his body quickly warmed it.

He pulled the brim of his hat low over his forehead to give Cass and Bonner as little as possible to recognize. He got busy fixing their quick breakfast.

Kate was back in the blankets by the time he had the food ready. He served her plate and coffee cup there. "I'd better take a couple of blankets and put them over there," he said. "They'd smell a rat right away if it looked like we'd spent the night together. They'd hardly believe my story of you being my saddle pard."

"Well, didn't we? And aren't we?" she asked coyly, encouraging Ryerson with her pluck; she was clearly no longer frightened by the prospect of taking on the pair of killers.

Ryerson grinned in response. "We did and you are, Katie, but I don't particularly care to announce it to them."

They ate quickly, watching the land to the north, and managed to spend the time by polishing off the coffee that had stayed warm overnight. The sun was already high.

"They say coffee isn't good until you can float a pistol in it," he said. "This stuff would qualify."

"Do you hear me complaining?"

"Well," Ryerson said, "I hope they show up soon. It'd be a damn-fool stunt if they'd somehow ride wide of us and we'd lose this advantage." His breath caught. He'd hardly spoken the words before two riders topped the knoll and started down its grassy slope toward them, a remuda of four horses trailing behind. Kate quickly pulled the blankets over her.

"The moment of truth," he whispered. "You're sleeping off a drunk. I'll make out like I'm a little wobbly, too. When I mention Leander's name, you kick off those blankets and come out of them with the shotgun cocked. I'll have Pat's six-gun trained on them."

Persuaded that Cass and Bonner could not yet see them that well, he leaned down, pulled back the blanket, looked at her questioning face, kissed it, and pulled the blanket back over her. "You don't mind my using your husband's name?"

"Good as any," she said, her voice muffled by the blanket. She lay still.

Ryerson pulled the tall collar of the trail coat higher around his neck, the tips of it curving past his cheeks. He ambled to the blazing, smoky fire, picked up a cup and squatted, pretending to take his ease. While they were still at a distance, he lifted the tail of the coat to free his two pistols. He doubted if the exposed gun butts would spook the pair; there was nothing odd in this country about a man being on the alert.

From what he knew of Bonner's taking the lead, Ryerson pegged him as the large, grim-faced man riding ahead. Cass rode slightly back, managing the rope that held their small herd strung together. Ryerson warmed his hands at the fire, making certain his fingers were limber when he went for his gun.

"They're still a quarter mile away," he called softly to the woman huddled under the blanket. He knew she lay tense, holding the shotgun carefully with both hammers at full cock. He studied the blanketed form as he spoke. There was no movement nor response. She was a game one.

As he watched the approaching pair from this distance, they seemed to spy him and his fire. They stopped to talk before veering toward the camp. Soon Ryerson could hear and feel the drumming of hooves on the packed earth under him. Bonner, still in the lead, was a big man with a dirty, hairy face and a short, thick neck; his head seemed to sprout from his shoulders. He bulked in the saddle, looking almost as big as the horse he rode. A slouch hat, the broad brim turned down, shaded and nearly covered his face. His large lump of nose pushed out of a thick and full beard. Above the nose, an oval of exposed cheekbones and forehead was broken by bushy brows over squinted black eyes that roved the scene as the two rode in. Evil glinted in Bonner's eyes; Ryerson could see it even at this distance.

Cass appeared to be built about the same, giving his horse no small task to carry the great hulk of flesh and bone. Cass's eyes had a less sinister cast. Ryerson thought he would be an easy man to buffalo, either with words or with a gun. Bonner, on the other hand, looked like a man who would fight tough and die hard.

Ryerson spied his horse in the string. It hadn't been cared for in three or four days. He was anxious to get it back—another reason for his trap to work.

Ryerson crouched close to his fire, trying to appear casual and only half interested in the pair riding toward him.

"Howdy," Bonner called as he halted with an air of apprehension about twenty-five yards from the camp.

"H'loo," Ryerson sang out cheerfully, not moving from his crouch. "Appears you're up and about early this mornin'."

Bonner edged his horse in closer, his eyes taking in the camp, sizing up the situation. I'd hate to drill him where he sits, Ryerson thought, but if I have to, I will.

"We got a sight of travelin' to do this day," Bonner said. He was close enough now that his voice was less of a yell. Cass came up alongside him, still controlling the horse string.

Ryerson put down the cup and began to get up, weaving a bit as he did. When he straighted, he held a palm against his cheek and grimaced. "Whoo!" he said. "Doesn't do to get up too fast. My pard and me put away some coffin varnish last evenin', and you know what that can do to a man."

"You got any coffee?"

"Finished the last of it just now. Fresh out. Didn't expect company way out here. My pard'll howl when he wakes up. He ain't worth a hoot in the morning without his coffee, and with the head he'll have, he's gonna be a bear."

"Any of that whiskey left?"

"Nah. We ain't got but little of anything. Running low on grub, too. Any towns north of here?"

"Only a bunch of shacks that calls itself a town.

Patchknife. A way out west of here there's a place called Medicine Springs."

"Any ranches?"

"Some," Bonner said.

"Me and my pard's lookin' for work."

"Them critters yours?" Bonner asked.

Ryerson cranked his head around slowly, as though it hurt, and looked at the two draft horses and then back at Bonner. "Them two? Yeah. Like I told you, we ain't living too high off the hog these days. That's all that's left of a little jerkline outfit we had in Arizona. There ain't no work out that way. Oh, lots of work, but then you got the devil's own time collecting your wages. You know. Everybody's broke these days. Why don't you and your friend get down?"

"Like I told you, mister, we got a piece of ground to cover this day. Bound for Texas. Was hopin' you'd have a drink or at least some coffee."

"Well, I'm going to start some fatback and some beans here in a shake. You're welcome to share what little we've got."

Bonner looked back at Cass. "We ain't et yet, Lacey," Cass said.

Bonner studied Ryerson, still sizing him up. Evil men, Ryerson thought, were usually suspicious men, and Bonner was no exception. "Take them hosses off yonder and hobble 'em, Sam," Bonner said finally. "We gonna take this gent up on his offer. But then we got to git."

Ryerson almost gasped. He'd figured to keep the two together. With them separated, if anything went wrong with Bonner by the fire and Cass in the field, things might go badly. He figured to play a patient game until Cass came back.

"You wouldn't have any coffee, would you, mister?" Ryerson asked. "It'd sit awful well with breakfast."

"We got nothin'," Bonner responded. "Been on the

road most of a week, and set out none too well provisioned as it was. Mostly we been eating jackrabbits."

"There's a few of them around, that's for sure," Ryerson said. "But a man's truly up against it when he has to start gnawin' them."

"That's us," Bonner said. He eased out of the saddle, hitting the ground heavily with a grunt. Cass turned and led the horses away from camp.

"The name's Geer," Ryerson said. "Harold Geer."

Bonner only grunted again and came to the fire to crouch and ram his cold-stiffened fingers close to the flames. He flexed them as the joints warmed.

"Them horses of yours," Bonner said. "They look better broke to a manure wagon than to the saddle."

"They ain't the best and that's a fact," Ryerson said. "But me and my pard have run into a string of bad luck. That's why we're headed up this way, lookin' for work."

"All the way from Arizona? Huh." Bonner grunted again. He eyed Ryerson as though not fully convinced. It was getting close. Ryerson's heart thumped. He was relieved when Cass got the horses secured and stumped stiffly back to camp, rubbing his hands to get the blood moving, his walk uneven from joints tight with the cold, though he had been in the saddle little more than an hour. Cass came up to crouch beside Bonner and began warming his hands.

Ryerson felt his assurance coming back; now I've got them, he thought. He moved, as if limbering stiff muscles himself, to flank them slightly when he made his play and to allow Kate free traverse when she swung up the shotgun. If there was gunplay, he wanted to be out of range of those deadly barrels. Crouched as they were, Bonner and Cass would have a tough time going for their guns.

"We could swap horses with you," Bonner said, watching Ryerson move about. Suspicion appeared to grow in his eyes. Ryerson figured he'd better not delay too long. "There's a couple of good ponies in our string," Bonner continued. "Three of 'em got saddles, and two even has rifles and gear in the saddlebags we'd throw in. A couple men got killed up in Patchknife and we bought the horses out of their estate, you might say. What we paid put those men in the ground. Their outfits was all they had."

"I've known a few like that," Ryerson said. "We sure could use better mounts." He kept the talk light, waiting for the right moment to strike. He hoped Kate would be patient. He also did not like the suspicious glint that continued to reappear in Lacey Bonner's eyes.

"Kinda strange," Bonner said, and Ryerson's heart skipped. "You fellers in need of good riding horses and we, you might say, bein' overstocked. Almost too good. You wouldn't have to come up with much boot. We could probably peddle those two of yours to some rancher down the line. Somebody'd sure be lookin' for a couple of good draft animals."

Bonner was shrewd. Ryerson figured any second he'd smell a rat about the horses. At this point Bonner wouldn't bat an eye over killing simply on a hunch. Any minute he'd wonder why all the talk and ruckus hadn't wakened the sleeping "cowpoke."

"What would you have to have for a pair of horses?" he inquired.

Bonner looked again at Kate's workhorses. "I'd have to see them better, but just offhand, I'd say give us twenty dollars and take your pick for you and your pard from our string. I'll throw in the saddles and rifles."

Ryerson chuckled. "My pal and me hardly got thirty cents between us. Ten dollars tops. Otherwise, I think we better keep what we got till we can get jobs and trade 'em. There's a man up there, somewhere around that place you call Patchknife, that's lookin' for a couple of hands."

Bonner and Cass both looked at him. "That so?" Bonner asked. "And who might that be, Geer? We just left jobs up there." The edge of suspicion grew stronger in his voice.

"Oh, I can't think of his name just now," Ryerson said, pausing as if puzzled, hoping the trend of his words would alert Kate. "My pard there, he knows it. Let's see. Ah, yeah! It's ... ah ... Leander Folsom!"

He called the name loudly and deliberately, taking Bonner and Cass off guard. In a flash he had his gun free and poised. Out of the corner of his eye he saw the blanket fly free as Kate came up with both barrels trained on the two and a serious glint in her eye.

"Hold it right there!" Ryerson yelled, watching their eyes. Cass and Bonner stiffened, eyes darting with realization. They wisely had not moved out of their crouches by the fire, but looked angrily at the pair standing over them now and at the hardware pointed at them.

"I'm a son of a bitch!" Bonner growled, his eyes turning mean on Ryerson and then swinging back to Kate. "Nobody'd be riding workhorses way out here. Hell! Should've got the drop on you first and then asked questions. Damn you, Sam, you was the one wanted to come over here!"

"Well, hell, don't go blamin' me for everything," Cass whined. "Hey, Lacey, ain't she—"

"Yeah," Ryerson growled. "That's her. That's the woman that put the buckshot over the cabin door a couple nights ago after you'd killed her man. If she'd done the job right, all this would be unnecessary."

14

Ryerson suddenly felt his mood swinging from jubilation at having pulled off his trap of Cass and Bonner to a controlled disgust and fury with the pair in his grip. The man of honor in him wrestled with his vengeful beast to keep from shooting them down on the spot. That would be the easiest.

Pat Graydon's murder had cut deeply, and his anger over the brutality of it surged back as he watched the pair submit to the guns held on them while their eyes registered racing thoughts of how to escape. A grief that had grown less painful with the presence of Kate Folsom emerged again in all its bitterness. Now he had them to contend with, in spite of taking them without firing a shot. At this moment he hated them, ached to be rid of the responsibility they represented.

But it was a job that had to be seen through to the end. He was certain there'd be more ugliness before he got them to justice in Patchknife. They'd be balky as mules going back up the trail, and would have to be watched every step of the way. If either of them worked free of the ropes he put on while Kate watched with her shotgun, and got hold of a gun themselves, it would be over for him and Kate.

Going back up the trail surely held some new confrontation with the Antrims. They would cross his trail or catch up with him.

Fatigue suddenly ground him down more than ever; the next few days, he realized with a depressed, sinking feeling, were not going to be a Sunday school picnic. In most ways, he was glad Kate was with him, to share the responsibility of getting them back for trial. But she was a woman, an attractive one at that, and Bonner and Cass had already done something vicious and fatal to one woman; they'd also tried to have their way with Kate. Ryerson couldn't be exactly certain she wouldn't cave in and be an extra burden—a hazard in itself—when he finally came up against the Antrims. Nah, he thought, not Kate, and then he hoped his reassurances weren't whistling in a darkened graveyard.

"I suppose you're the waddy we seen with Graydon a couple of days ago." Bonner's words represented a harsh intrusion, a gruff rasp grating against the irritations Ryerson already felt. He resented them even trying to make small talk.

"Just before you low-lifes gunned him down." Ryerson's words were clipped and impatient. He couldn't resist; it was the only answer in him.

Ryerson was not altogether gentle as he cinched up the pair; he battled to keep his own rage in check at being this close to Graydon's murderers. With Kate's shotgun on them, he roped their wrists tightly, but with enough slack for them to mount and handle a horse.

"Sam was the one done that," Bonner tattled. "He damn near won a long-range shootin' contest once. Got him a good eye for a rifle." Ryerson stiffened; Bonner talked as if gunning down Pat Graydon was akin to a good shot on an antelope.

"You got a big mouth, Lacey," Cass said. "How

'bout I tell 'em whose idea it was to go back and clean old Antrim's plow and get the woman down?"

Before Bonner could react, Ryerson spoke up, measuring his words to keep his tone level. "No matter," he said. "You'll both hang just as high for what you've done. Since we're keepin' score, which of you did in this lady's husband?"

Kate hadn't seen Leander's murder. Ryerson watched her, gauging her reaction. She kept the shotgun level; her eyes revealed no sign of weakness or revenge as she searched their faces.

"That was—" Cass started. "Go to hell, Geer."

"It isn't Geer anyway," Ryerson said. "It's Ryerson. Which is of no great concern one way or the other. As to who pulled the trigger, that, too, is of no great concern. The jury won't distinguish between the two of you. You'll be side by side when the hangman drops the trap. That's the only thought right now that keeps me going."

"What you figurin' to do with us?"

Ryerson looked at Kate, wondering at her feelings. The free and open conversations between them were over, at least for a time. Until they were rid of Cass and Bonner, what they had to say to each other would be strictly business. That, in itself, was an aggravation.

"You ought to have it figured. We're headed for Patchknife. I'll get you there, provided you behave yourselves. And if the Antrims don't give us too much trouble. That's what's going to take some doing."

"I knew those bastards would be after us," Bonner said. "Where are they?"

Ryerson wondered if he was being too cordial with the pair. Every time he looked at them, his mind recoiled with the dark memory of that startling crack of rifle fire splitting the silence, and of Pat Graydon going down in a flailing heap beside the buffalo wallow. He struggled to keep his voice calm. "The Antrims? I hope they're still walking back to their ranch minus their boots. By the way, you've taken care of their horses for the last three days."

"So that's where them cayuses came from!" Cass said. "We wondered why Graydon was draggin' along such a remuda."

At the mention of the name again, Ryerson gritted his teeth. "It would be a hell of a lot easier on me if the Antrims had gotten you first. I'm bound by law. No, something ever stronger than law. I'm bound by a vow over the body of the man you killed from dry gulch, to take you in. So you'd better not figure on anything sneaky. I didn't know those other people, the Antrims nor Mr. Folsom. That lady's scattergun is holding you accountable for Leander Folsom. The Antrim boys only want to get even for Matt and their sister-in-law. Me, if I'm forced to lay you low with my old Navy or Pat's single-action, the last thing you'll hear before your lights go out will be Graydon's name."

Neither man responded, but watched Ryerson solemnly. "By the way," he said, "Graydon deputized me before we left Patchknife. He needn't have done it, for I'm a federal officer out of Fort Walker, New Mexico. Either way, it's my duty to place you under arrest for the murders of Matt and Stella Antrim, Patrick Graydon and Leander Folsom."

"Well, ain't we gettin' to be the high-and-mighty one," Bonner snarled angrily. "So I suppose it's my duty, Mr. Lawman, to tell the judge we didn't do any of that stuff you're talking about." He growled his final words. "You got no witnesses, Ryerson."

Fury welled out of Ryerson like a red tide. He backhanded Bonner across the mouth. The surprised killer brought up his trussed hands to massage the pain and blood from his lips.

"She's a witness against you for Leander Folsom, and I am for Pat Graydon," Ryerson screamed.

Bonner was right back in anger. "Our word against

yours, and I reckon I'll also have me a talk with the judge about you cuffin' us around." His lips curled in pain and his own rage. "One thing a lawman don't do is rough up his prisoners, particular all hog-tied thisaway."

"Don't tempt me, Bonner." Ryerson's voice was level in his cold fury. "I'll be much better off if I leave your carcasses out here for the buzzards and the varmints, the way you did Pat Graydon. That, or hand you over to the Antrims when they ride us down."

Kate moved closer to the three at the fire, lowering the shotgun now that Cass and Bonner were secured. She had stayed out of it, only speaking now to break the tension. "Cole, I think it's time we fixed a proper breakfast. We probably ought to feed them, too."

Ryerson looked at her again, knowing his anger flashed in his eyes, but powerless to cope with it; it was that strong in him. He only hoped she wouldn't misread the signs of his change in attitude and think any of his outrage was directed at her.

"Huh!" he responded with a grunt. "I suppose we are obligated to keep them fed. For all I care, they can starve. But it is up to the state to see to the welfare of murderers before they are executed, and just now we're the state, since the law enforcement has passed to me."

Kate got busy pulling together food and utensils to fix a meal. Ryerson added sticks to the night's embers, keeping an eye on his prisoners. They sat subdued by the fire, now and then glaring at each other like punished schoolboys passing blame for getting caught in the melon patch.

Bonner was silent a long time. When he spoke, it was an angry snarl that did nothing to endear him to Ryerson. "You said your name's Ryerson?"

Ryerson looked at Bonner, despising him. "That's it."

"Cole Ryerson, ain't it? The woman called you by your first name."

"What if she did? You're Lacey Bonner and he's Sam Cass. This is hardly time for formal introductions, and I'm not especially enjoying the pleasure of your company."

Bonner ignored the slur. "I heard of you before, that's all. Long time ago. Sam and me spent some time in New Mexico. 'Boot Hill Cole' cuts a pretty wide swath down there, I been told."

"Spent time in New Mexico, eh?" Ryerson growled back. "Pity you didn't do time, maybe in a place like Yuma Territorial Prison. Might've taught you something. On the other hand, it probably wouldn't have, knowing you."

"Judas, you got a mouth on you! You're sure a bigger damned fool than the stories they tell about you down in the border country. Hear tell it you're *muy hombre*. Now that I see you and hear your mouth, that's horse puckey. You're a fool, a damned big one at that."

Ryerson became interested in what was on Bonner's mind. "Now there's the pot calling the kettle black. What are you driving at?"

"The Antrims. I know what's on their mind, and about what they'll do to you and sis there to get at me and Sam. You're well on your way back to New Mexico, Ryerson. You got you a damned good-looking woman to ride with you now, fix your vittles and tend to a man's needs. You could let us go and nobody'd be the wiser. You can even have the extra horses."

"Watch it, Bonner. You're getting close to stepping out of line again. And that's the level you operate on, isn't it? I'm in this now to see you taken in to stand trial for murder, one of them a friend of mine."

"And die tryin' when the Antrims get hold of you,

I suppose. You figure me and Sam are worth dyin' for? A couple of old saddle bums?"

"Uh-uh!" Ryerson's anger was on the rise again. "You two aren't worth the rope they'll string you up with. It has to do with honor, which you wouldn't understand if I was to talk myself blue in the face."

"Honor!? Ha ha ha. You hear that, Sammy? Honor! That's what he's all about, takin' us in. Honor! To hell with you and your honor, Ryerson. I'm here to bet since you started riding with the widow lady yonder, you been on 'er more'n a little. That kind of 'on 'er.' Yeah, that's what it's all about. Like a damned fly, you're stickin' around for the kind of meat that's the sweetest!"

Bonner's lewd remark stung. In an instant Ryerson, who had been standing, bent into a fast crouch and backhanded another cuff at Bonner's head, spinning him from his squat by the fire and sending the two of them, roped together as they were, sprawling into the crackling firepit, scattering embers and dumping a skillet of salt pork Kate had frying.

The two instinctively recoiled from the flames and leaped up, trying frantically to brush and beat the sparks from their wool clothing with their tied hands. Both sputtered strings of foul language and glared at Ryerson with murderous looks.

"Cole!" Kate yelled in sudden astonishment at his rage.

"Dammit!" Ryerson screamed at her, sensing his voice rising out of control and shrill with the fury boiling out of him. "I don't see how I'm going to get to Patchknife with these two, even if we don't have to fight our way through the Antrims!"

He spun on his heel, shoving his hands, which trembled to be at their throats, into his hip pockets. He strode away from the camp to be rid of the hateful predicament a moment. He stood silently, his back to them, the distant blue mountains a serene backdrop to the scene of his anger. He felt his body tight and quivering with animal rage that yearned in the worst kind of way to get out of him.

From here on, in addition to two unwilling and potentially vicious prisoners, and the deadly Antrims waiting for him up north, he would have to fight himself every step of the way to keep from killing his charges the minute they stepped out of line again.

Maybe Bonner was right, he thought; maybe I ought to turn them loose and take Kate and ride to New Mexico.

❖ 15 ❖

Ryerson looked around at the camp as the other three mounted up; it marked a turning point in the manhunt, and he was still in a dark mood.

"Cass! Bonner!" He called to them sharply. The two studied him sullenly, their roped wrists clutching saddle horns for support. "Get it through your thick skulls once and for all. We are going to Patchknife, come hell or high water, and I expect we'll encounter a large portion of both. You will improve the trip greatly by going along willingly. Balk and buck and try to escape and you will only make it tougher on yourselves."

He had decided that he and Kate would each lead one of their horses for added security. The riderless horses were strung together by lead ropes, all secured to Cass's horse.

"Go to hell, Ryerson," Bonner muttered through gritted teeth.

"I expected that out of you, Bonner. I've told you where I stand. My orders are clear. Any questions?"

"Yeah. What the hell do you expect us to do all snubbed down thisaway after the Antrims gun you down? You and your lady friend there?"

Ryerson stared at Bonner, his exasperation rising. "The Antrims are not going to 'gun me down.' I'm taking you in, whether or not we meet up with them. Get that through your head, too."

"We're all going to be the same in their eyes, and you know it. So, Mr. Ryerson, you better figure on staying awake and keeping eyes in the back of your head. Sam and me'll skedaddle the minute you ain't looking. Even if you got us roped up, you'll never know when them Antrim boys'll come sneakin' in."

Ryerson studied Kate, and spoke to her. "I've thought about that. If these two get away from us, we'll have to start all over. This isn't going to be an easy trip. I've got an idea that will help."

He walked to where Kate sat watching him from Graydon's horse. "Give me Pat's rope there," he said.

Puzzled, Kate worked free the hemp lariat held by thongs to Pat's saddle and handed it to him. Slipping out his sheath knife, Ryerson cut two generous lengths, coiled the remainder and handed the loops back to her. He walked to where Bonner watched him quizzically from horseback. Ryerson tied one end of the line around Bonner's booted ankle. "What the hell you doin', Ryerson?!" Bonner demanded.

"I just remembered a couple of guards I had. Your horses. You'll see."

He tightly knotted the other end of the rope to Bonner's stirrup and began to do the same with Cass.

"Hey!" Bonner yelled. "You can't do that!"

"And you can't tell me to go to hell either, mister! Now you've got three ways to die. The hangman's rope in Patchknife, or hung upside down over that half-wit Myles Antrim's slow fire. That, by the way, in case you hadn't heard, is what they have planned for you."

Cass watched him intently as he secured his foot to the stirrup. "What's the third?"

"Right here, Cass," Ryerson said, feeling a sense of

total command. "If you or your pard there get muley or try some kind of funny stuff, all I do is fire my Navy and spook your horses. I don't have to tell you what will happen if you get dumped out of the saddle on a stampeding horse."

"You miserable skunk," Bonner muttered, still grating his words through clenched teeth.

"Next time you decide to tell me to go to hell, Bonner, I'll figure a fourth way for you to die."

"You ain't even human," Cass said.

"And I suppose you are," Ryerson said, hooking a toe into his own stirrup and hoisting himself into the saddle. He realized when he hit the familiar hump of leather-covered wooden saddletree how good it felt— to be back astride his own horse. It was like climbing back into your own familiar bed after an absence, or bellying up to a friendly, oft-frequented table. It added to his heady feeling of command—of himself and of the situation.

"Ever see what happens to a man dragged by a horse running wild?" He asked it loudly, more or less at the three of them.

The expression that passed between Cass and Bonner showed that they were only too aware of what he was talking about. Ryerson felt he really had them now.

"Move 'em out!" he called, kneeing his horse and swinging him north. Not caring that his two prisoners watched, he blew a kiss to Kate Folsom. "Keep that scattergun handy, Kate. One false move from them, fire that thing off, straight up. Don't even bother to shoot them. Their horses will do the rest."

He glanced at her. In full accord now with his attitude toward the prisoners, Kate winked and grinned and ducked her head in acknowledgment. That, too, was a spur to his spirits. As they rode out, Kate held the reins in her left hand, bracing the shotgun's butt in a businesslike way against her thigh with her right.

The same hand held the lead rein to Cass's horse. To Ryerson, Kate was a picture of grim determination, and his heart made itself known to him with its proud fullness in his chest.

He figured if he had to lose Pat Graydon, Kate Folsom was a suitable replacement.

As their prisoners' horses picked up the choppy canter, the faces of the murderers were set as they bounced awkwardly, a frosty fear burning in their eyes while they clutched their saddle horns for dear life. They were both well-aware of the consequences if they lost their balance.

Ryerson had led out, pulling Bonner's horse but not looking back. He knew Bonner was there, hands clenched and white. Kate rode near Bonner, almost abreast.

"Now for act two of the plan," Ryerson called back to her. "Avoid the Antrims."

"How do we do that, Cole?"

"Next stop, Tom Moon Dog's station. We're going back to Patchknife the long way. Unless Mitch Antrim anticipated that kind of move, we'll pass way east of them. If they find Pat's burial and open it to see what's in it, they'll drive due south, figuring I'm the only thing now standing between them and our friends here."

"They'll probably stop at my place."

"And see Leander's fresh grave and you gone. Probably figure you headed for Patchknife. We'll be northbound, but some distance to the west, and they'll continue probing south. With luck, we'll pass in opposite directions but miles apart."

The morning had not warmed much after daylight. The sun was up and walking its slow westward course over the sky. While it shone down yellow on the four travelers in the high plains, they felt a tension and an uneasiness in the air around them. Ryerson wondered at it. This day was different, somehow, from the mornings before. He swung his eyes from watching the trail ahead to the mountains. A color of old ashes hovered along the peaks like campfire smoke on a still morning. Sullen was the word—like the mood of his prisoners. Throughout his trip in this country, the mountains to the west had been a pretty sight to behold, something to inspire a man when he looked up at them. It was bellwether to the mood of the land. Now they bulked ominously and hostile, a threat and a danger clinging in their dark presence.

Nasty weather was building up there, he thought. In the lead spot in the party, he had time and opportunity for his mind and his eyes to work. The man riding point always found himself in that situation. In this case, his eyes always had to be on the alert. He could not make bold assumptions about what had happened to the Antrims. He could not afford to drop his guard only because he thought he had effectively put them briefly out of the race for vengeance against Cass and Bonner. Best also, Ryerson thought, not to trust hunches and rash judgment where Cass and Bonner were concerned; that pair had filled a few graves around Patchknife, and Lord knew what other evil lurked in their past lives.

He swung his head in a check of his prisoners and Kate. Looking back at the sullen color over the mountains, his mind worked on that word, weather. If it was good, men said that. It was good weather, or nice weather. When it turned ugly, as it appeared to do now in the dark pall that hung over the mountains, or with wind signaling the approach of a storm, or the quiet chill coming on the land in early winter promising big flakes at first and then a curtain of small, bitter ones that robbed a man of warmth and visibility, then men spoke more often than not only of "weather."

"There's a spell of weather coming," he'd heard them say when the skies were fixing up to dump an unholy mess down on a bunch of men caught in the open. And now he saw it, over the mountains. A spell of weather coming.

At first the ashen sky simply seeped farther down the great slopes. Then the gray coldness of it streaked earthward in slanting rays that obscured the peaks and the great uplifts of rock and earth with their trees and scrub growth. In the distance it did not resemble rain or water, but only jagged, stringy tendrils falling out of the foggy thickness toward the peaks. It rained down a hell of a rain over there.

Around the four riders the growing wind at first fitfully tossed the tops of sage and mesquite and whipped the pinion and juniper and combed the grass with random fingers.

To the west the clouds rolled, wind-rumpled, and came in to merge over the riders and blot out the sun. The land abruptly turned from yellow sunlight to a dismal gray almost as he watched, the weather darkening it and cutting down his visibility. Quickly the storm moved in to surround them. Ryerson could not imagine where dust could come from in a land so thick with grass, and yet here it came, lifting and sifting out of the west on a wind that now caught clothing and buffeted it and flipped up hat brims and snapped them down to whip against temples.

Conscious of movement behind him, Ryerson looked back to see Bonner working with restricted hands to screw his shapeless hat farther down his head for fear of losing it altogether. The windborne sand stung the four riders and their mounts, working its grit into mouths and ears and eyes. Against the wind, Bonner's mouth made words when he saw Ryerson watching him.

"You miserable bastard," his lips said, soundless against the wind's howl. Ryerson only grinned, delighted with the big killer's discomfort. The storm of swirling dust didn't last long, but the wind kept up. Ryerson's hand was slapped by a big blob of water slanting in on the wind. One pelted his nose; against the roiling heat and the dust, it felt good, and he stuck his tongue out to taste and test it. He felt drops the same size start to drum on his hat.

It became time for slickers. He swung his arm up for a halt. His horse's tail twitched as the raindrops hit it like a host of horseflies. Ryerson slid down, shouting at Kate to dig out her rubberized poncho while he guarded Cass and Bonner. Without a word she worked free the rain gear behind her saddle and shrugged into it. He did the same while drops came closer together and the hiss of rain grew louder. Signaling her to watch the prisoners, Ryerson untied Bonner's slicker and, getting back on his horse, rode up beside the angry-looking big man and worked the coat over his shoulders without allowing him to get his restrained arms into the sleeves. He secured several buttons while Bonner's arms, outstretched for the saddle horn, remained unprotected.

"We're in for a regular blue norther," Bonner yelled at him over the roar of rain. "You gonna leave us like this?"

"Naw," Ryerson sneered. "I'm going to turn you loose and take you over to that nice, snug hotel yonder and get you a warm room out of the wet."

Sure that Bonner would try nothing under the circumstances, he rode to Cass's side and began working free the saddle thongs holding his "fish." To the north and west of them a spectacular splinter of dazzling lightning pierced the darkness, making a sudden, crackling sound all its own. In a moment the thunder growled in about the same place, the rolling noise quickly growing into a sudden, booming bark that shook the ground around them and as quickly went back to its growling. The giant thunderclap had filled the sky with a slamming roar as though something powerfully heavy had been dropped in heaven.

Sam Cass trembled as Ryerson worked the slicker,

shawl-like, around his restricted shoulders, the rubber sleeves flapping uselessly. Ryerson grinned again. The big guy feared lightning and was as afraid of thunder's booming racket as a small boy.

"Don't worry, Cass," Ryerson shouted over the storm's cacophony. "They say you never hear the one that gets you!" Cass's fear-blanched face was almost comical as his wide, unblinking eyes searched Ryerson's in childish terror.

Clearly, Ryerson was delighted that his prisoners were uneasy.

16

The rain slanted in on them in helter-skelter torrents, pummeling their bodies with the fury of a woman scorned. Ryerson turned up his slicker collar against it and hunched close to his horse, water cascading off his hat brim. The hat was quickly rendered a sodden mass and the brim lost its curl, drooping as it shed noisy water down on his shoulders, back, and chest, protected by his waterproof coat. With his head bent, his face was not as severely pounded by the wind-driven drops that pelted the rest of him like hurled buckshot.

Still, splattered water bounced around and hit his face; he licked at it as it cascaded over his upper lip, and he blinked against the drops that ricocheted into his eyes. Water sponged and trickled through his luxuriant four-day mat of beard.

The horses marched resolutely and stoically into the storm, heads down, the riders miserably damp and isolated from each other in the roar and wet. They were all equally miserable now.

Around Ryerson the wind whipped the huge raindrops, scattering them every which way. Though it had started as a light hiss, the rain now roared, the sound drumming annoyingly at his ears and beating the ground under the horses' hooves.

He had little fear that his animal would be dirty after its many days without attention. Its hide and hair were drenched, soaked through, washed and rinsed. Visibility narrowed to a few feet, and Ryerson only urged his mount in a direction he considered would be north by instinct, knowing Kate would follow, dragging Cass's horse and the rest of the string. Ryerson still clutched the lead reins of Bonner's horse as he gripped his own with hands soaked, dripping, and turning stiff with cold.

The driving wind continued to howl around him, breaking in great barks of sound, whistling and spitting rain into his face and drenching his booted legs, unprotected by the slicker. Randomly the sky was still rent with roaring peals of thunder; he did not look up at the crashes of splintered lightning around him.

Though he had a firm grip on Bonner's reins, Ryerson stiffened in sudden horror as he felt resistance on the lines. The leather reins, turned slick and gummy in the rain, abruptly tensed and sang slithering through his cold-clenched hands and fingers like a slimy snake. In vain he tried to hold the line as it slipped out of his grip.

Instantly alert, Ryerson arced his head around through the wall of water. Either at a command from Bonner or in sudden panic, the outlaw's horse had made a lunging stop, jerking the reins from Ryerson's hands.

Seeing his chance despite his lack of control, Bonner clutched the saddle horn tighter and put spur to his horse's flanks, urging the drenched animal into a gallop. Ryerson's reaction was as fast, swinging his mount around to give chase. Bonner's horse leaped away at a right angle to the route they had taken and quickly began to lose shape in the thick wall of rain. At his abrupt spur, Ryerson's horse reared, forelegs pawing, and lunged after the fleeing Bonner. Ryerson caught a blurred glance of Kate's gaping face as he wheeled past with no time to confer. She had kept the shotgun muzzles down, out of the rain, but now leveled them on the man she guarded. Ryerson only briefly saw Cass as a sodden, dark hulk of slicker in the saddle, his drooping hat brim covering most of his face. As he sped away from them, he heard Kate's shout of surprise. He shot a quick glance back over his shoulder at the string of horses becoming unsettled by the sudden flurry of movement around them, and Kate's attempts to control them.

Swinging around, Ryerson rode straight into the teeth of the storm, the driven rain lashing his face with the burning sting of whipping tree branches. Drops splattered into his eyes fully, making it all but impossible for a clear view of the retreating Bonner, but knowing that Bonner, too, had trouble seeing.

Bonner made tracks in any direction away from his captors, his only control being that of the speed of his horse—as fast as he could urge the animal on—despite the threat of injury or death by dragging if he tumbled off. Ryerson rode in a similar fear that he himself would go down if his horse slipped in flooded, uneven ground that now was a layer of mud as slick as greased glass.

Obviously, the giant that Ryerson chased had chosen this means of risking death in an escape try rather than being tortured to death by the Antrims or being dropped into eternity at the end of a hangman's rope.

Racing pell-mell, Bonner's horse was on a panic run. Ryerson, in concern for life and limb, did not let his horse out to race at the same top speed, but held him in check, traveling only fast enough to keep the fugitive in sight through the blinding wall of rain. Though running erratically, Bonner's horse stretched the distance, the rain still pouring over them in ugly gusts. The roaring water drowned out any sound, soaking the land around the two riders and isolating them in this breakneck race.

Bonner's horse neared a low rise of ground and, making a beeline in the direction it had taken, rolled up the grade, losing momentum as it went, its rider bouncing clumsily on its back, hands still frozen to the saddle horn, out of control.

Ryerson made up time by veering around the base of the low knoll, and was much closer to Bonner's runaway when the horse and rider bounced down the far side to again hit a top-speed stride into the flats. The animal nearly went down when it hit a small pond of pooled rainwater, slipping and sliding and sending up geysers of splashing liquid mud.

Ryerson could see that the land leveled out as he urged his horse after Bonner. He drew closer now, letting his horse have its head in the more predictable terrain. It became little more than a horse race, Bonner crouched low against the horse's neck, gripping the horn and kneeing the horse to an even faster pace. Bonner did not need to look around to know that Ryerson was quickly closing the gap.

Only for a moment did Ryerson think of unleashing his Navy to bring down the horse or its rider. Either way he would have an even greater mess on his hands. He would continue to try to ride the outlaw down. Gradually the distance narrowed between the two flying horses, as the roar of the wind and dashed raindrops howled into Ryerson's face. His horse's head drew up even with the tail of Bonner's mount. Then he was alongside him. Bonner looked over, fury stamped in his anger-clenched face, gleaming with rain. His long hair seeped over his forehead and ears and was plastered to his head, giving him even more the look of a crazed and desperate man.

Bonner's free leg was on Ryerson's side. With no other means of defense, he pulled his foot free of the stirrup, trying wildly to ward off Ryerson's horse by kicking it away. Unbalanced this way, his hands lost their grip on the rain-slick horn. Ryerson saw him abruptly bounce out of the saddle, cling briefly behind it, and then lurch and roll away, falling off the stirrup that held him to the horse.

As Ryerson watched in disbelief, Bonner bounced heavily into the mud and drenched grass with a splash and a thump, inches away from the galloping, flailing hoofs. Ryerson wheeled his horse past the rear of Bonner's to be on Bonner's side as the man skidded like a fast-moving log, plowing a wake of muddy water behind him. Over the roar of the elements, Ryerson heard Bonner bellowing in terror.

Dragged, bounced, and bruised unmercifully over the rough, uneven ground, Bonner fought futilely to pull himself up by his clothing and body to get at the leg secured to the stirrup, his slicker a ripped, pulled-up, and rumpled mess enshrouding his body and making the task all but impossible.

Ryerson thought fleetingly of trying to get close enough to Bonner's horse to cut the rope or the stirrup. But then the bouncing, dragged body would be in double jeopardy from the flying hoofs of both horses. Ryerson really didn't care if Bonner died—but not this way.

If he tried something foolish like leaping into Bonner's saddle to halt the animal, he himself might fall and lose both horses as well as his captive.

Instead, he held back and crossed behind the horse with its dragged burden. He spurred his horse through the mushy grass alongside Bonner's animal. He caught hold of the bridle and slowly brought the heaving, prancing animal to a stop, its panicked, dancing hoofs still menacing the battered man on the ground.

In a sudden and new level of quiet without the thunder of racing hoofs, as Ryerson's lungs heaved and his heart pounded, the rain continued to pour down on the two sodden, breathless horses and men buried in the vastness of a prairie soaked to capacity.

The muddied and bloodied hulk of Lacey Bonner stretched full-length beside his horse, his foot and leg angled up, immobilized by the stirrup. His other leg was awkwardly drawn up under his body.

The rain poured straight down now, less whipped by the wind, settling into a downpour. Ryerson imagined that Bonner had been knocked cold; the hammering rain, he thought, would soon revive the man—if he weren't already dead.

Ryerson caught hold of Bonner's reins and got down, also clutching his own. Certain he had a tight grip on both, he walked to where Bonner lay, his face and body still pelted, his clothing a ruin of mud and water and abuse as he had been dragged. Ryerson crouched over the inert mound of what was left of Lacey Bonner.

Bonner had rolled and twisted several times in the dragging, sometimes on his back, sometimes on his stomach. His face was a mask of mottled grime and blood that the streams of rain quickly rinsed away. Ryerson saw that most of the blood came from a split lip and a ragged, clawed abrasion on one cheekbone. The crimson blood starkly defined other minor wounds against the filth of the man's relaxed face.

As Ryerson crouched and watched, Bonner's eyelids flickered and opened and he looked up with a pained, angry expression at the man bending over him.

"Ryerson," he said, his words more choked grunts. "Son . . . bitch."

"Well," Ryerson said, "you had to play the damned fool, didn't you? I see that busted mouth of yours didn't put a crimp in your foul language. I'll give you a minute to get your wits back and we'll get going again."

"You got to help me."

Now it was Ryerson's turn for foul talk. "Bull ... shit!"

"Then hold that horse still."

"I'd ought to let him drag you back."

"Goddamn you for a heartless son of a bitch, Ryerson." Bonner still lay unmoving, the tension of his body saying that every bone and muscle ached. It also said that Lacey Bonner was mad—mad clear through.

"Where you're concerned I am."

Painfully, awkwardly, with one leg secured, Bonner got his free one out from under him and bounced and boosted himself to a one-legged standing position, and reaching for the saddle horn with tied and muddy hands, pulled himself with a low groan into the saddle.

Ryerson swung himself up on his horse's back, holding Bonner's reins. He tried to get his bearings against the gray pall of rain that obscured everything except what was close at hand.

He was lost. The mountains to the west, his only true direction finder, were lost in the curtain of rain, mist, and low-hanging clouds. Momentarily he calculated. They had been riding north. When Bonner bolted, the horse had plunged away generally westward. Ryerson sensed that in their run, they had veered slightly south again.

He mounted, brought their horses around and started back in a direction he only had a hunch was right, guided by instinct. He calculated that their run had been no more than a mile from where he had left Kate and Cass.

In this country and with the limited visibility posed by the weather, a mile in any direction but the right one would put him miles from Kate. He let instinct guide him. It seemed right and good, the way he led them. He felt more assured when, after what seemed a long time of poking through the veil of rain, he came to what he remembered as the hill Bonner's horse had fled over.

It would be only a short distance more. If Kate had stayed where he left her, he should be able to see their horses soon. The rain appeared to slacken.

He had no definite guide as to where she might be. He found no sign of her. He rode past the knoll in a route that seemed right and true, plagued by the thought that the horse string he left with Kate had become unsettled by Bonner's hasty action. Ryerson called into the gray wall of water still seething around him. "Kaa-ate! Hailoo, Kate!"

It was along in here, somewhere, he was sure, that Bonner's horse had bolted. He squinted, trying to see through the thick stuff. The rain let up, settling into a heavy drizzle, the visibility improving.

The land stretching away from him on all sides still dripped with the now fuzzy, indistinct rainfall that brought a chill with it. Ryerson looked around, still trying to be sure of his bearings.

Though the steady drip that now looked as though it would last all day, the form of the mountains, about where he expected them, began to take shape, looming a dismal gray out of the rain and mist.

Ryerson's gaze fell on Bonner behind him, seeing a smug sort of smirk flit across the battered, filthy face. Bonner's features were puffy, as though he'd been in a fight.

Ryerson felt anger rise in him again. It wasn't enough that he'd had to split away from Kate to chase this brute halfway across the territory. Now Bonner was taking fiendish delight in his dilemma.

"Stick that grin in a can, Bonner, and stopper it up."

"Whatsa matter, heap scout? Lose your lady friend? What'll you do now for poontang?"

Ryerson's first impulse was to ride up alongside Bonner and kick him out of the saddle to be dragged some more. He was worried about Kate. She must be somewhere out ahead, hauled there by the briefly spooked horses. He'd catch up with her very soon, he was sure.

Instead of taking out his frustration on Bonner, Ryerson angrily reefed on Bonner's reins and rode on, moving north by northwest again. Kate knew this country, knew the way to the stage road and on to Tom Moon Dog's stage station. Surely they'd meet there, if not before.

Feeling his anger and anxieties ride out of him with the jolt of his horse's pace, Ryerson bent low over the saddle horn and let it rain.

❖ 17 ❖

A day later the land had dried and the clean, cottony froth of cumulus of Ryerson's first days in this country clung again over the mountains. Ryerson by now figured he must be nearing the stage road and a direct route to the stage station.

Abruptly any mystery surrounding Kate Folsom's disappearance was gruesomely cleared up. She was in the hands of the Antrims.

In a grove much like the one in which Pat Graydon died, they found the tormented body of Sam Cass. Myles Antrim's wish had come true. Cass had been suspended on a rope over a fire and had his brains fried like scrambled eggs.

The Antrims had left the body hanging when they rode on, probably with Kate in tow as their prisoner and hostage. Cass's face was beyond recognition, his head a charred and scorched nub of black. His slicker, which he still wore when they pulled him up feet first, had hung down to melt to bright yellow taffylike tatters. It also probably concentrated the fire's heat on the agonized man. The foul odor of death lay on the air thick as old rancid grease in a skillet. The body of

Sam Cass was nothing short of a mess when the Antrims got through with him.

He hung like a man crucified upside down, arms outstretched but still tied, feet together, the body doing slow pirouettes in the soft breeze off the mountains.

Sam Cass must have had plenty of time to beg for mercy as Myles increased the fire's intensity. Kate was probably forced to witness the torture, and Ryerson shuddered with the thought of it. What a hell of a thing to have happen to that fine woman.

Bonner, who had been mouthy since the pair of them had been alone, turned deadly serious in the shock of the spectacle of his saddle pard. "Aw, God, Ryerson! Don't let 'em do that to me!" he pleaded shrilly.

Ryerson had seen death in many ugly ways in four years of combat service, and a great many more as a lawman, but he had never quite become callous about it. Watching the corpse do its slow twirling upside-down dance in the desolate and taut silence of the high plains, he felt the pinch of nausea like a fist squeezing deep in his gut. The sensation passed quickly and disappeared with Bonner's almost whimpered plea. Anger rose again. Ryerson's concern, really, was for the welfare of Kate Folsom, and he held Bonner responsible.

"If you hadn't pulled that funny stuff back there yesterday, I probably could have prevented this from happening to your partner."

He pondered it. His situation had now worsened by enormous degrees. The Antrims had Kate and surely planned to bargain with him to trade Bonner for her. Because of that prospect, Ryerson was sure, Kate Folsom's body did not dangle alongside that of Sam Cass. In the unreality of sudden rage, Ryerson vowed that if they'd harmed her, he'd give them the same treatment they gave Cass.

He took a deep breath and sighed it out, despite the burned, choking stench of the body still some distance from them as they sat their horses and stared at it. Ryerson found himself in some fine mess. To save Kate, unless he pulled off a miracle, he might have to turn Bonner over to them.

"Well, Bonner," Ryerson said finally, "he was your pard. We've got no shovel to bury him with. I'll turn you loose under guard if you'll cut him down and fix him up under some rocks the way I had to do with Pat Graydon."

"No, Ryerson!" Bonner recoiled in horror. "Don't make me touch him!"

Ryerson shook his head in bewilderment. "Yeah. That's about as far as loyalty and friendship go with the likes of you, isn't it? It's a cinch I'm not up to building another rock pile, particularly around one of his breed."

"You just going to leave him?"

"Of all the low-life scum! You aren't man enough to mess your hands with the body of your friend, but you want me to do the dirty work. You begin to sound like a churchgoing do-gooder."

"Aw, Ryerson, hang the talk. Let's get out of here. The looks of him hangin' up there makes my skin crawl. Get me to Patchknife before those damned Antrims show up again."

"You know something, Bonner? God above and the Devil below, neither one has a word for the likes of you. There hangs a man, your friend, and even at that, any shred of decency escapes you. Have you got to piss or anything?"

"Whattaya mean by that? Sure, I could stand to get down off this horse and stretch my legs. Let's do that and then let's get riding the hell out of here."

Ryerson eyed his captive angrily and spoke coldly. "I'll tell you what. You stay in the saddle and piss in your pants. I'm going to snub your horse to those trees where Sam's hanging so you'll have to watch. I'm going to cut him down myself, after all, and put big rocks over him. Despite what he was, Sam Cass was once a human being—some mother's son—and I can't ride away from that obligation, as ugly and repulsive as that job is."

Bonner was clearly relieved, but still worried. "Come on, Ryerson. Let's go. The Antrims—"

"Uh-uh. They're long gone. It'll be good for you to be the witness. And while I'm doing it, I want you to think on something else. They have Kate Folsom, probably with the idea that they'll try to bargain with me to trade her for you."

"You wouldn't let them do that!?"

"All you've been able to do for two days, Bonner, is remind me how much I miss the 'widow woman' and how important it is for me to get her back safely. Think on that. Right now, you're small potatoes in all this."

Because of the way Sam Cass died, Ryerson's task of covering the body was more grisly than building the cairn for Pat Graydon. Ryerson had done the first one in deep grief and respect that an old friend have a proper and safe resting place.

He hurried at the chore with Cass. The body was even more hateful in death because of the mess that had been made of it. Ryerson said little to Bonner as he went about the hard work of hauling in rocks and piling them to cover the body.

The gruesome job done, the pair of them started out on an angle to the mountains, hoping along here to cut the trail of the stage road.

Ryerson figured by this time he had to be due west of the Folsom ranch, but he had no way of knowing how many miles. Abruptly, like seeing an old friend in a crowd, the road appeared—a wide and rutted ribbon of dust and potholes cutting through the rolling grasslands. Out of the south it came, bearing northwest by north, scribing a straight line in the direction to what must be Medicine Springs.

Though it aimed to point true, the road dipped and twisted around hills and rocks and other natural diversions and obstacles in the land. Finding the road at last was something of a relief, but it also spoke with threat and apprehension for what was to come. Ryerson was that much closer to the out-for-blood confrontation with the Antrims and the chancy job of getting Kate out unharmed, and Bonner on to Patchknife and jail.

Neither was the impact of at last finding the road lost on Bonner, who had been subdued in the ride from the place of his partner's death. Out of the trackless prairie and with the road under him, Bonner spoke, his voice husky with the slightest tremor of emotion. It said that he knew that soon he might meet the men who had done in his partner and wanted nothing more than to do the same for him.

His voice almost had a fawning quality. "Why ain't we going straight into Patchknife? You know the Antrims are out this way, don't you?"

Ryerson looked at his prisoner, struck suddenly with an odd feeling of pity. Bonner looked smaller, weak and vulnerable and bent in the saddle, like one who had suddenly aged twenty years. Here was a man with some evil kind of guts to abuse and gun down helpless people in cold blood. Now he knew he faced death from the hangman's noose or worse, at the hands of the Antrim brothers. Lacey Bonner, clearly, was scared to death.

For once, in spite of himself, Cole Ryerson was openly candid with the ruthless killer.

"I figure the Antrims will make for the stage station. It's the last place I really want to go, but I seem to lose my options by the hour. There's probably food there, and we can get fresh mounts if we need them."

"I don't want to go there."

Ryerson ignored him, and only thought out loud.

"If they're there, maybe something can be worked out. They got half of what they set out for—killed your best friend. Maybe with that, they've had enough blood. Hell, I don't know. The law still has to deal with that. They're in hot water now for sure, and they know it. They probably also know that Pat Graydon is dead and that it's just me standing in their way to get at you."

Bonner's whine was annoyingly insistent. "Then what the hell are we going there for? Let's swing north to Patchknife. Let them bring the woman there. They won't hurt her, Ryerson."

Ryerson held nothing but contempt for cowardice in any form. If he hadn't known it before, Bonner's reaction to finding Cass reinforced his opinion of Lacey Bonner; he lacked totally any shred of decency or courage. An edge of anger flared in Ryerson.

"Your chances of getting to Patchknife and to fair and impartial justice are going to be better, mister, if you get inclined to go along with my plans and my actions. Either way, you've got no choice in the matter. But we'll both stand a better chance of getting you through safely if you play along. Fight me and what I need to do, and I guarantee you it'll go a hell of a lot tougher on you than it will on me."

"We could make it past them, wherever they are, Ryerson. It's a big country."

"Sure, and leave Mrs. Folsom to their tender, loving care. No. Bonner, there's going to be a showdown with the Antrims before I get you to Patchknife no matter how I try to get back there with you. No point in shying from it. If they're at Moon Dog's station and I don't show up in a reasonable time, Lord knows what they might do to her before getting back on my trail. No, my friend, we're going right in there, and somehow I'll face up to them."

"You don't know them. Don't know what they'll do."

"I don't? And I suppose you do? Who was it piled rocks around your pard, a man they lynched in the worst possible way? Huh! Don't tell me, Bonner, about not knowing the Antrims. To top it off, I humiliated them some nights back, and I'm the one that got in the way of their getting to you and Cass, and they're not about to forget that. They've got the same fate planned for the two of us, Lacey, sure as God made the sun to shine."

"So you figure you can talk to them? That's pretty damned dumb on your part, Ryerson, you know that." Bonner had turned testy again.

"Right now, any step I take in any direction, I'm damned. I figure maybe there's a better chance talking with them at the stage station than there is on the open range and them riding us down with blood in their eye and murder in their hearts. Either way I'm damned. We're both damned."

"I got your answer for ya."

"Well, Mr. Lacey Bonner, if you have an easy out for this untenable situation, as the military would say, please share your thoughts."

"Easy. Turn me loose. Give me the head start it takes for you to get there. Tell the Antrims anything. Tell them I got away from you back there in the rain. Hell, Ryerson, the last the woman saw, you were chasing me. You're the only one that'll know, and your skin'll be saved. The Antrims'll have to believe you. Chances are they'll forget you just like that and come tearin' down in the country after me. I'm the one taking the risks that way, facing them in open country. You'll be out of it, you and the woman. One night in that shack of hers ought to make it all worthwhile."

Ryerson pondered Bonner's proposal; there was merit in the idea, but not enough. "Tempting, Bonner. Mighty tempting. But it won't work."

"Why not, for God's sake? Why are you so bullheaded in the face of certain death?"

"It comes under the heading of living. With myself. At the risk of sounding lofty, it has to do with that thing called honor that we talked about. Something you're not too familiar with."

"Of all the ... That's what it's all about? Honor?"

"Rhymes with Bonner, but that's where the similarity ends. That's as plainly and as simply as I can put it to a man like you. Remember, you made fun of honor a day or so ago."

Bonner turned thoughtful, even a bit downcast. "Yeah."

"We've lived our lives differently, you and me. You've ridden roughshod over anything and everything to get what you've wanted all your life. What you couldn't get any other way, you killed for. So there's no point in trying to beat into your thick skull what makes a man take risks for the side of right. There's no use bandying the point. We're going in and face up to them. Like men. Cowardice respects guts. That may be our only hope. Don't worry. The only way they'll get to you is over my dead body. Again, that sounds stupid to you. You're a hell of a cause to die for, Lacey Bonner, but that may be the way it'll turn out."

"So why do it, for God's sake? Let your damned sense of honor slip a little for once. Let me go and save your hide. No point in your dying, and your way is certain death for both of us. My way gives us both a chance at living."

Ryerson had no more chance to think it through. He first heard the fleshy whump of sound and the sudden muscle tug and quiver of shock race like a telegraphed message through the horse under him. The horse shied and bucked away from the impact, legs crumpling. Blood spewed from a high neck wound behind the ears, and Ryerson was splattered with the sudden gush of its release.

Knowing instinctively that the horse was finished, though trying bravely to regain its footing, Ryerson rolled out of the saddle away from the direction his mount lurched. He hit the ground running, but quickly checked his run. The distant rifle's report, a muffled crack, drifted to his ears to be recorded briefly in the haste to make sense of the sudden action.

Ryerson bounced back to the horse as it went down in a leg-flailing cloud of dust, jerking in death that had come in an instant. He wrenched his Winchester from its boot and leaped to use the quivering horse as a shield against the next round that was sure to come. The bullet had been intended for him, but hit well ahead of its mark.

With the abrupt noise and confusion, Bonner's horse reared and plunged away, the rider taking quick advantage of his opening for freedom.

"Bonner!" Ryerson shouted, but Bonner made no move to check his horse's flight. Keeping low to avoid another shot from the unknown ambusher, Ryerson knelt from the cover of his horse and thumbed back the Winchester's hammer, feeling the cold, businesslike tension of the rifle's trigger under his finger. He aimed at the head of the retreating horse, almost obscured in a wake of dust, and led the animal in his sights, being coolly careful to avoid wounding or killing Bonner.

As he knelt, another bullet from ambush seared the air behind his head. The report of his own rifle drowned out its clipped whine. Bonner's horse, dead from a bullet in the brain, dropped head first, front legs buckling and skidding down in its own dust cloud. Off balance, Bonner pitched out of the saddle to land heavily in the dirt, stunned by the fall.

Ryerson dropped back behind the cover of his own dead horse to turn his attention to his assailant, sensing that at least for a few moments, Lacey Bonner would present no problem.

The land that had suddenly brought forth so much roar and violence quieted quickly, an eerie silence settling over Ryerson as he watched and waited for more from ambush. Only the low moan of ground wind, combing the grass near him, intruded on the hollow silence.

As he crouched out of breath, waiting for his lungs and his heart to return to normal rhythm, Ryerson's nostrils grew aware of the familiar smell of horse sweat of the animal he crouched behind, and of the unfamiliar smell of profuse blood from the wound that had killed the animal. He was also aware of the warm, musty smell of the bruised grass and dirt under him.

In this moment of peak danger, all of his senses tuned themselves to a razor's edge.

18

Ryerson studied the land around him. There was no natural escape route, and the day still had hours to dark; no obvious means to pull back, circle around out of sight and blind-side or confront the bushwhacker. He figured he could cringe here like a field mouse behind his dead horse for long, hot hours before night would shield him enough to make a move.

Bonner would come to at any minute and could get away. But Ryerson knew that the Antrims wanted Bonner dead more than they did him. Still, he knew the bullets were meant for him, to get him out of the way. They hoped to save Bonner for the same horrible fate they had meted out to Sam Cass.

Realization began to dawn on Ryerson as he crouched, rifle at the ready, against the carcass of his horse, which was already taking on the stale smell of death, the body lifeless, the once-vibrant muscles stiffening against his own body.

There was only one gunman. If the three Antrims were out there, why hadn't there been more rifle fire?

Ryerson's instinct told him there was but one rifleman. Had the Antrims split up, sending Mort out to fire from ambush? Thinking it out, he figured that was unlikely. Mitch, who called all the shots for the brothers, surely would not have left the others and come out alone. Assuredly it was not a job they would trust to Myles.

None of this squared with his impressions of Mitch Antrim and the twins. Since the second bullet had sailed in at him as he fired to kill Bonner's horse, the air around them had turned quiet; no more shots. That, too, was unsettling. The Antrims would be impatient to get at the fun of roasting Bonner's skull; they would have filled the land with lead to drive Ryerson into some rash action, to risk exposure and sudden death.

Ryerson glanced toward where Bonner's horse lay, a full fifty yards from his position, a bulk of duncolored death in the tall, waving, and hot grass. As Ryerson watched, Bonner stirred groggily and rose up on hands and knees, staying that way for a long moment, head down, getting back his senses. Ryerson could see that the huge bear of a man slowly swayed and arced his head to rid it of the splinters of befuddlement slammed into it by the jarring fall.

If Bonner got up, he'd be the target of the assassin's bullet. Ryerson knew that if he tried to reach Bonner, he'd have to sprint across fifty yards of open country fully exposed—sure to take a bullet at some point during the run.

He stiffened in frustration. All the way along, this had been a mixed-up venture, and what had happened in the last few minutes was typical of the way it had gone all along. Time and again since he had set out from Patchknife with Pat Graydon, he'd had to risk his neck for the sake of justice.

Maybe he ought to let that dumb Bonner raise himself up, he thought, muddled as Bonner was, and take a bullet from out there and be done with it. Still, Ryerson knew he could not willingly allow that. As he watched, puzzled by this latest chain of events, Bonner stupidly dragged himself to the mound of his dead horse, pulled himself up and perched on the hump of rib cage and belly.

"Bonner!" he screamed across the distance separating them. "Stay down!" Right now the dry gulcher was surely leveling his sights on the broad back of Lacey Bonner. He wasn't that certain that the Antrims would kill Bonner any way they could even if it meant depriving Myles of his depraved delights. Still no shots came as Bonner leaned upright in the hot sun against the dead horse, groggily trying to grasp reality after being knocked cold. He perched there like a man mentally counting his fingers and toes to make sure all of them were attached.

In the heavy silence it became plain to Ryerson that whoever was out there was after him and not Bonner. Ryerson's mind raced. What the hell, he thought wildly, was going on?

Any minute Bonner would get his senses back, untie his leg from the stirrup and lumber away into the grass, and possibly take a bullet as he tried to escape. A sprint to where Bonner sat dazed would be sheer madness. It would draw fresh fire; the ambusher so far had clearly indicated that he had in mind only to kill Cole Ryerson.

Still, Ryerson thought, it would at least precipitate some kind of action, even if he did take a bullet—and he just might. The man out there in hiding, whoever he was, was not a good marksman. He had proved that in hitting the horse and not him, and then missing the second opportunity when Ryerson had knelt rock-firm to take a sight on Bonner's retreating horse.

Looking at it from that angle, Ryerson thought, the odds were in his favor if he made himself a moving target. He slid his hand alongside the dead horse's ribs to his saddlebags and sought out his extra box of cartridges for the Winchester. If this proved to be a long standoff, he might need them close at hand.

The six chambers of his Navy were loaded with caps, powder and balls, the hammer resting securely on the small pin between the percussion nipples. Six rounds were all he really needed for close-in work. Pat Graydon's rig, which proved cumbersome when worn with the Navy, was carefully rolled and stowed in his other saddlebag.

Before he jumped up to race to Bonner, Ryerson decided on one last stunt, an old time-worn trick, but it still sometimes fooled even the best of them. He perched his hat on his rifle muzzle and carefully inched it above the dead animal. That fast, he heard the whump of bullet tear into the dirt ahead of the horse, followed in split seconds by the distant rifle's report.

Crouched out of sight, Ryerson couldn't tell if the bullet had clipped to the right or left of the hat, but surely the rifleman hadn't plotted proper elevation for the distance. The bullet, he calculated, must have landed two or three feet low; he wasn't up against a terribly formidable adversary—at least as far as long-range shooting was concerned. Maybe they had sent Myles out here after all. Ryerson's confidence flowed back.

Jamming his unmarred hat back on, he gripped his rifle firmly and again checked the ground to where Bonner still leaned against his horse. Bonner's broad back was exposed to the same rifle fire he himself was taking, but none of it was directed Bonner's way. Ryerson inched out, crouching to take full advantage of his barricade until the last second. Then, coming erect, he lunged full-tilt toward Bonner. It was not far, and Ryerson felt himself fill with euphoria and confidence as he pounded out the distance, feeling his boots beat against the hard earth and the air rushing past his face. A bullet tore with a thud into the dirt several feet behind him, again too low to be effective. Not only couldn't his assailant judge his rifle's proper elevation, he was also unable to accurately lead his quarry—another key element in long-distance shooting at a moving target.

Ryerson felt himself grinning with superiority as he covered the ground at top speed; he knew now that only one man was out there in the hills.

With his second shot at the running Ryerson, the shooter began to get his range, the bullet thudding closer, but still not in a threatening zone. Ryerson raced up to Bonner, threw an armlock around the big man's neck and bodily bowled him over to drop behind the cover of the dead horse. Ryerson's nose was keen on the sharp odor of old and new sweat on Bonner's body.

The giant murderer still tried to collect his wits. Ryerson flopped beside Bonner, ready to restrain him if he tried to jump up again. "Somebody's out there trying to kill us," Bonner said dumbly, his thinking still clouded from his heavy tumble off the horse, his second in several days. "They shot your horse, Ryerson, and then they shot mine. Now they'll ride us down and take us off somewhere and string us up like they did Sam and burn us alive. You've got to do something. Ryerson! I don't want to die like that!"

"Oh, God, Bonner, stop your damned whining! There's only one man out there. He didn't shoot your horse. I did. To stop you!" Bonner looked at him curiously as they made themselves as small as possible behind Bonner's dead horse.

"But—"

"Damn you, Bonner! Don't play your dumb games with me! You saw your chance to skedaddle again."

"I couldn't control him. I thought you was dead. I don't want the Antrims to get me."

"You knew damned well I wasn't hit. I've committed too much and lost too much in this now to let you ride out. Another dumb stunt on your part. We both could have gotten out of here on your horse. But no.

You and your bonehead plays. Better get it through your head, mister. Without me, you're dead meat—in the worst kind of way. There's always a chance for you in a court of law. You'll have none—zero—against the Antrims. You keep fighting me, and I'll guarantee you that one of these times you'll make good your escape from me and ride right into their hands. Then you'll howl for me to protect you, only I won't be there!"

Bonner's eyes were less distant; he was coming around, but acted as though he hadn't heard Ryerson's words. "Mitch and them are out there trying to get us."

"No they're not. There's only one man out there, and for some reason he's not after you. At least he doesn't want to kill you outright. All those bullets have been meant for me. It's not like the Antrims to split up."

Bonner's thinking cleared. "So how do you figure it, Ryerson?"

Ryerson thought about it. It was risky as hell. He knew he couldn't trust Bonner. He'd have to chance it. "We can't get out of this spot and go up there after him as long as it's light. We have to make him come to us."

"Oh, sure, Ryerson. Just stand up and yell at him to come on over for some coffee and a smoke, I suppose."

"Something like that." Ryerson grunted a chuckle and grinned at Bonner. "I sure could stand a little of both; take the rough edges off things."

"Why, you're crazier than that harebrain Myles Antrim."

"Whoever is out there knows I'll risk a lot to keep you in custody. Now listen and listen good, and do what you're told. Or I will shoot you down and be done with all this and walk out of here scot-free. With you dead, the threat to me is over. Get that?! As long as you're alive, that guy is out there to get me out of the way so he can get to you. Once you're dead, his reason for killing me is gone. So don't tempt me, friend." Ryerson was bluffing Bonner; he had other plans.

"Whataya want me to do?"

"Make a break for it. Pretend to. I'll cut you loose from the horse and take the ropes off your hands. We'll jump up and make like we're fighting. You'll get in a good lick and knock me down. Then you make a break for it. I guarantee you he won't shoot at you. I'll give you a little head start before I get up and take a shot at you. Believe me, I won't hit you. You fall down and play dead. I'll run out to you, and when I do, he'll take a shot at me. As long as he doesn't know if you're dead or alive, he wants me dead. I'll make it close to you before I fall. He'll think he got me, but from what I know of his shooting, the bullet will only fall in the grass and won't kick up much dust. He won't know he missed, but I'll be down."

"What if he don't miss?"

"If I'm wounded and out of it, or dead, you're on your own."

"That's a hell of a risk. But what then?"

"If I'm not hit, I'll be near you. We lay still till the guy comes out to see. He won't ride in. Makes too good a target. He'll walk. Then I'll get the drop on him. Whoever he is, he'll probably want to take scalps back or something ... I begin to sense the hand of a scalper in this."

"The Antrims only want to cook our heads."

"I mean an Indian. They never had enough cartridges to get too good, particularly long-range shooting. I'm sure the Antrims are better shots."

"Nah, there ain't no Indians around here anymore. This is cattle country. They've run most of those people to reservations or shipped 'em off somewheres else."

Ryerson didn't pursue it. "You ready to do what I said?"

"You'll probably shoot me anyway—to save your own damned hide."

"If I had in mind to do that, you've given me a hundred chances and even more reasons these last few days. We've got no choice. We've got to find out who this guy is and what he's after."

A glint came in Bonner's eye, and Ryerson stiffened. Sometimes the eyes spoke greater truths than the mouth. Ryerson readied himself for more of Bonner's treachery. "Let's do it," Bonner said.

"All right. Now." Ryerson unsheathed his knife and cut Bonner free. Bonner rose up and stepped away from the dead horse. Ryerson waited a short moment before getting up to grapple with him. There was no pretending when Bonner lunged at him, and Ryerson realized he'd made another foolish mistake in trusting Bonner the least bit; he played for keeps.

But Ryerson was ready for it. Bonner fought as though he meant business, but had surmised that Ryerson would only play-act. Ryerson struggled against the big man's weight and power as they wrestled for the advantage. "You low-life Judas," Ryerson grunted as they struggled, the sweat pouring from both of them as their bodies strained in the muggy heat.

Bonner was incredibly strong. Ryerson was no match for the brute strength of the man. He managed to break away from Bonner's bear hug and plowed a right into his midsection, hearing a whoof of pain.

Ryerson didn't see it coming. Bonner, in reeling back, lashed out a haymaker that caught Ryerson on the cheekbone, and for a moment his lights went out as he sprawled flat on his back. As he shook his head to clear his vision, he saw Bonner race away.

Furious at the double-cross, Ryerson jumped up and

RYERSON'S MANHUNT

again loped after Bonner, almost immediately catching up and overtaking the man lumbering away like an ox; Bonner was no high-speed runner. At least here, Ryerson thought, I've got the advantage. He hurled himself at Bonner, his arms encircling the pummeling legs; Bonner went down heavily.

Preparing to give the hulking brute no advantage this time, Ryerson leaped up, spun out his Navy and brought it down with a vengeance on top of the already tender head of Bonner, who clumsily tried to pull himself up. Bonner went down like a dropped sack of grain, out of it again.

Maybe, Ryerson thought, this time he'll be out of action long enough not to mess things up until I can attend to the man in the hills. Thinking fast, Ryerson stood over Bonner, again making himself a target. It wasn't long in coming. When the anticipated bullet smacked into the dirt a few feet from him, Ryerson hurled himself to the ground in a heap as close as possible to the stunned outlaw. Now if only Bonner will stay out of it a while, he thought, trying to lie perfectly still despite the uncomfortable position and the itchy sweat on his back and chest, this little stunt may lure the bushwhacker out here.

He clutched his Navy in a sweaty palm, its six good rounds still in the cylinder. If it came to a showdown, he'd need only one of them.

19

Lying there, almost breathless with his struggle and his anxiety for what the next few minutes would bring, Ryerson had ample time to remember that the sun was always hottest at the tag end of the day. It would yet be several hours before the intensity of it would dull as the great orange globe settled west of the mountains and its dwindling light and heat came at him in slanting rays.

The sun had barely begun to angle to the west, and still beat on him intensely.

Ryerson fell with his body pointing west, making sure his gun arm was free, extended in front of him. When the man came at him, as Ryerson was certain he would, all he had to do was raise the gun arm slightly to take the man by surprise.

Fortunately, Bonner lay still, and Ryerson was far enough from the big brute that he couldn't listen for Bonner's breathing. The Navy's clout on his head, after the shock of the fall from his horse and all his other abuse these last few days, may have done the man in, but Ryerson doubted it. Bonner's skull was simply too thick to be fazed by a gun-barrel tap.

A half hour ticked off by Ryerson's calculation. His

muscles cramped in the uncomfortable position. The ground was hot, the grass steamy beside him. If his life hadn't depended on lying as still as a dead man, he would have squirmed to stretch himself into a less awkward position. But he knew he was being watched from afar.

The sound of footsteps drifted softly to Ryerson. Or maybe at first it was only the sensation of sound. Ryerson tried to tune his ears to distinguish only that sound and ignore the soft rubbing of the wind against the grass. No, he was certain; someone was out there, walking carefully through the grass, gun at the ready, coming up to check on the pair of men sprawled apparently lifeless under a relentless sun.

Ryerson grew aware that the man had an irregular cadence to his walk. One step was firm and confident. The next was soft, a shortened pace, as though the man favored a bad leg. Ryerson was confident it was not an Antrim unless he had been wounded.

Through slitted eyes under a hat brim askew on his head in his fall, Ryerson watched the man come up to him, the top of his head appearing first over the grass that obscured Ryerson's vision. Then thick, wide shoulders came into view and Ryerson saw a trim waist and a gait impeded by a stiff leg. Ryerson breathed lightly, waiting.

His assailant wore the working clothes of a cowboy, a sun-faded and threadbare blue cotton shirt and Levi's jeans the sun had been at work on as well. The faded cleanliness of the man's outfit suggested he was more than a saddle bum of the Lacey Bonner ilk. Even though his clothing was commonplace and worn, they suggested pride on the part of the man who was in them; his clothing fit him well.

Ryerson could not be sure from the approaching footsteps that the man was not wearing moccasins instead of riding boots.

Ryerson also saw that the man who he suspected to

be Tom Moon Dog wore a broad and flat-brimmed hat with a low, rounded crown fitted straight and tight to his head—a style more traditional to the old mountain men and passed along to their Indian friends, rather than the rakish styles adopted by the cowboys. Beneath that hat brim Ryerson could see the tight-slitted and sinister eyes of an Apache—eyes that seemed to perch above prominent cheekbones in a craggy face that could have been described as handsome if it were not so set in a constant scowl. Moon Dog's luxuriant black hair was chopped close to his neck and ears after the fashion of the white man. The exposed skin of his hands and face carried the rich, weathered color of mahogany.

Moon Dog carefully approached the two men in the grass, his lever-action Winchester at port, ready to swing it to his shoulder and fire instantly if either man showed a flicker of life. He wore no six-gun, though Ryerson suspected that Moon Dog wore a good-sized bowie against his right rear flank.

Slowly, like a lazy snake, Ryerson raised his clutched Navy and sent a round tearing through the tensed hush around them with a roar like a dynamite explosion. The shot went well wide of the approaching Tom Moon Dog. In surprise, the Indian planted his feet and began to swing down the Winchester's muzzle, the roar of Ryerson's round quickly losing itself in the hot, heavy air.

"That was a warning, Moon Dog," Ryerson shouted, certain that he'd made the proper identification. Pat Graydon said the Apache stage station manager had a game leg. Moon Dog somehow had to be tied to the Antrims. Ryerson only raised his head and his hand to show the Colt in his grip.

"Put the rifle down easy in the grass and walk over here!" Ryerson commanded.

For a long moment, without a word, Moon Dog studied Ryerson as he came out of his prone position to a crouch and then bounced to his feet, holding the Navy's muzzle level. Moon Dog pivoted only slightly to study the hulk of Lacey Bonner, inert in the grass.

"Don't worry," Ryerson said in a growl. "He's not dead. I told you to drop the Winchester and get over here!"

Moon Dog held the rifle in an easy grip, but at the ready. He knew that one misunderstood word and he was a dead man. His manner suggested he wouldn't try anything foolish.

"Better yet," Ryerson called in a commanding tone, "lever the rounds out of it and dry-fire it a couple of times at the sky to make sure it's empty." Moon Dog hesitated. *"Now!"* Ryerson screamed.

Like an obedient but rebellious child, not taking his eyes off Ryerson, Moon Dog crisply cranked out four rounds, working the action three or four more times. He hoisted the muzzle skyward and clicked the trigger. He levered and dry-fired it again before dropping the gun to his side and limping closer to where Ryerson stood beside Bonner's body. When he was near, Ryerson told him, "All right, now put the rifle down there." Moon Dog grudgingly obliged.

"You're Ryerson all right," Moon Dog said. The Apache's English was good, too good, uttered in a throaty bass that was distinctly Indian, his words precise and enunciated well. At one time or another, Ryerson surmised, this man had been in a reservation school and had taken well to white man's language.

"You knew who I was before you started shooting. You've got a lot of answering to do."

Moon Dog ignored Ryerson's remarks. "What about him?" He waved at the inert Bonner.

"Oh, he's not dead. He'll come around with a sore head any minute. What's the big idea trying to gun me down?"

Moon Dog still evaded him. "The Antrims sent me to find you."

"To commit murder, I suppose."

"They want that man."

"And, for some reason, you want me. Is my hunch correct that it has to do with a certain crippled Apache up here in this country, miles from his homeland?"

Moon Dog's eyes narrowed and glinted in an unspoken affirmative.

"You'll tell me sometime, I suspect. Meanwhile, you've certainly made a mess of it. You're out to kill me, and all that's come of it is that Bonner and I are unhorsed and it's at least thirty miles to your place."

"Twenty-five," Moon Dog said. "You killed Bonner's horse, not me."

"Look, we're making a lot of fool words. Get down to brass tacks. You're Apache. Graydon told me. With that bum leg, all you can do is work for the white man, and you work for him running the stage station. I take it that what you've got against me has something to do with your injury. Or at least with the old days." Ryerson's hard-edged anger was evident in his voice.

Again Moon Dog didn't acknowledge with words; his eyes spoke all that was necessary.

"I get it. It was the old days. You rode with Mongo. Or Little Pete."

"Little Pete."

"Oh-ho!" Ryerson exclaimed at the revelation. "One of Little Pete's warriors. That's how it happened. You know me from the old days when I was assigned to ride with the cavalry helping chase Little Pete all over the territory down near the border."

"Five years," Moon Dog growled, his words dripping with hate. "Five years I have been worthless to myself. The secret raid into Mexico that would have gotten your Major Hardcastle into serious trouble if it came to light. He and his blue-legs soldiers all but wiped out a village of Little Pete's band. You know, Ryerson. You were there."

"And, I suppose, so were you."

"My leg was ruined. I was one of the few survivors. Old men, women and children. All died. Hardcastle gave no quarter."

"It's small consolation, Moon Dog, but indeed I did report it. His evil scheming and some of his corrupt superiors caused my report to be disregarded. Major Lemuel Hardcastle got what was coming to him a year later. After a battle with Mongo. Hardcastle was secretly selling rifles and ammunition to the Apaches through intermediaries to keep the wars going and to gain favor for himself as a great war leader. He was put out of the Army without honor. Disgraced and banished. I helped get evidence against him."

A cynical half smile flitted across Moon Dog's face as though he sensed he was being lied to. "I did not see the man who fired the shot into my leg. I was told it was the marshal working as a scout for Hardcastle. The one they called 'Boot Hill Cole.' He was also known by another name. Ryerson."

"I get it," Ryerson said, his anger toward the crippled Apache mellowing. "All these years, every time your leg gave you pain, you thought of me and prayed for the day—this day—that you could get me in your sights or in knife range."

"Revenge," Moon Dog said. "It is a word I know well. I have thought that word many times."

"In spite of the fact that, like you, I operated as a soldier, or at least under Army orders, doing my duty, following those orders regardless of personal feelings." For the moment, Ryerson withheld the truth of his participation in the fight.

"You say that now. In the fight, you were in the thick of it, Ryerson!"

❖ 20 ❖

Ryerson felt his spirits slump lower than before on this manhunt as he studied his new prisoner and turned the events around in his head. Lacey Bonner at last hunched himself up into a sitting position and drew up his legs. He rested his elbows on his knees and buried his face in his great paws of hands and slowly rocked, fighting the pain in his head.

Ryerson dropped the Navy loosely into its holster and stood away from Moon Dog and Bonner so that if either made a threatening move, he could draw and get the drop on them in a split second. His mess was hardly getting better.

He was twenty-five miles from the stage station with two enemies, each with different reasons and different talents for getting him out of the way. One was a cripple and the other had had enough injuries to his head to be groggy and slow for the rest of the day.

Probably no more than one horse between them, and off somewhere a hell of a long stretch down a strange road, Kate Folsom was prisoner of the Antrims and at their mercy. The longer he delayed here, the greater were the chances that they'd do something to harm her—if they hadn't already.

"Come on, Bonner," he called. "On your feet. We've got some tall walking to do."

Bonner dropped his hands. His head rolled dumbly up at Ryerson. The man's eyes were bloodshot, the lids heavy, his cheeks and jowls puffy and discolored. Bonner's unkempt dark hair was pasted over his forehead in helter-skelter knots and snags thick with sweat and grime.

"Where we goin'?"

"Mr. Moon Dog here is going to lead us to his station."

Bonner's head cranked farther around for a long look, taking the measure of the Indian standing at bay a few feet away.

"The manager of the stage station down the road. The Antrims are there waiting for us."

Bonner seemed in so much pain, he didn't care. "We gotta walk?"

Ryerson looked at Moon Dog. "I don't suppose you came out here in a buggy or wagon."

The Indian's eyes were slits of hate. "My horse. Back there." He motioned with his thumb over his shoulder at the ridge of low hills to the west, where he had lain in ambush.

"Well, let's get moving. Nothing's getting done out here. Come on, Bonner."

"I can't. I'm too stove-in. I'm staying here."

"You are like hell! Get a wiggle on or I'll put a knot on the other side of your head and I'll haul you in tossed over Moon Dog's saddle. That or I'll drag you on the end of the rope like a side of beef."

Bonner knew Ryerson well enough by now. He struggled to his feet and began to stagger in the direction of the low hills. Ryerson looked at the two dead horses some distance apart and bulking like strange-colored rocks in the prairie grass. He'd have to come back for his saddle and gear later on. He picked up Moon Dog's Winchester, noting it was chambered for

.44, the same ammunition as his—and he still carried a full box in his shirt pocket. Moon Dog began his pained, shuffling walk after Bonner. If they were to make any time, Ryerson mused, Moon Dog would have to ride. Ryerson only hoped that the fog in Bonner's head would clear enough that he could make some good time afoot. It wasn't going to be easy. He strode up alongside the slow-moving Apache and timed his pace with his.

"Is the woman there? With the Antrims?"

"I should have killed you when I had the chance."

Ryerson's anger flared again. "All right. So you didn't. Now we move on to the next step. Is the woman with them!?"

"They came in yesterday morning."

"Dammit, man! Is she all right?"

Moon Dog scowled at Ryerson as if he wondered if he was required to give him the courtesy of an answer. "I don't believe they abused her, if that's what you mean."

Ryerson glanced at Bonner lumbering ahead, head down, plodding a directionless way toward the distant rolling hills. "You mean they haven't beaten her up. They haven't raped her."

"Those kind are like your friend up ahead. The woman looked very tired. I can't say what they did to her before they got there. They were only rude with their words and unkind toward her. All white men are alike. Mean to the helpless, but run when they meet their match. No sense of honor."

Ryerson's mind flashed on the arguments about the very subject he'd had with Bonner. He nearly grinned. He let it pass. "I know what kind of men they are. They sent you out here to find me. You probably didn't tell them you intended to kill me."

"I have a separate quarrel with Boot Hill Cole. They only want the one they call Bonner. Had I been successful, I would have had my revenge and had him to take back. All I want is for the Antrims to get what they want and get away from my place. I no longer seek to settle other men's troubles. I spent too many years as a warrior."

"Well, Mr. Moon Dog, I have very mixed feelings about that. I'd surely be happy to see you without trouble in your life, but not at the expense of mine."

"There's more to it. A stage also came in last night. Four passengers and the driver, an old man. The Antrims keep them prisoner, too. These are evil men, these Antrims. They think now they have more lives to use to persuade you to hand this Bonner over to them."

"And they sent you out to tell me this."

A compass needle in Moon Dog's head seemed to swing back and center on the most important thing on his mind. "Anytime between here and there, if I have the chance, I will kill you, Ryerson."

"And just where do you suppose that will put you?"

"The stage passengers will be free. Mrs. Folsom, who has been a good friend, she and her man, will be free to return to the grave of her murdered husband, and I will have the Antrims off my hands."

"And have your revenge."

"And have my revenge."

"And what then for you, Moon Dog?"

"This will all be over."

"Sorry, Moon Dog, not over. Your troubles will be just beginning. Kill me, sure. You'll have your revenge. You'll have Bonner to turn over to the Antrims and, as you say, get them off your hands. But what will you live with? You who talk of honor. Your honor, after all, is as hollow as the dead saguaro cactus skeleton. The Antrims intend to murder Bonner just as they murdered his partner, Cass, strung up head down over a slow fire."

Moon Dog set his strong jaw and stared straight ahead.

"What honor will you have after all that, Moon Dog?"

"Justice will be served."

"You can believe that? When you turn Bonner over to them to murder, you will become accessory before the fact, as they say in white man's law, not to speak of the charge of murdering me. Unfortunately for you, the white man's law, and not the law of the tribe, rules out here. If you kill me, the authorities will ask you the circumstances. If you tell the truth, you will be charged with murder and, sad as it is and disgraceful to me, white man's law will be even more severe toward an Indian. Or will you lie, Moon Dog, and then live with the lie the rest of your life."

Moon Dog looked straight ahead as they walked, not allowing himself to look Ryerson in the face. The muscles tensed and flexed in his strong, bronzed jaw.

"White man's law would see this man Bonner hang anyway. My law demands my revenge against you, Ryerson. I care nothing for white man's law."

"Yes, but now you live under its protection. You have taken the white man's way, his money, and you wear his clothing. Apache law here is the law of the outlaw. Kill me, and under white man's law you will be guilty of murder. You'll hang as high as Bonner."

"I will take you in to the Antrims. You will have the decision whether Bonner or five or six innocent people die. Maybe they will kill me, too, before you turn Bonner over. Or the woman. What is the price of your honor, Boot Hill Cole? My death? Her death?" Moon Dog paused and a silence passed between them as they walked, following the clumsy Bonner. "Maybe you will die in a fight with the Antrims," he said finally. "I wish it. Then I will have my revenge and *my* honor."

They had walked up the slow rolling grade of the first of the hills. Bonner had already caught sight of Moon Dog's horse hobbled deep in a grassy swale where it grazed. Bonner moved, almost stupidly, toward it.

"I don't mean to mock your injury, Moon Dog, but you will ride. I'll tie Bonner to your horse by a long line to make sure he won't lag. If you try to ride away, he'll be dragged. In his present condition, he'll probably die. The Antrims won't like you for that. They plan to watch him die ... slowly. By the way, I'll ask you for your knife, in case you get any ideas about cutting his line. Or throwing it at me when I'm not looking."

Moon Dog paused, and Ryerson swung an arm behind the Apache, yanked the long blade from its sheath and slid it into his boot top. Moon Dog took his total disarmament without emotion. "Too many things run against you, Ryerson," he said. "You'll never make it. Bonner, the Antrims, or me. One of us will get you, all for different reasons. I can no longer dance, but tomorrow I'll sing an old Apache song of rejoicing, of this I'm certain."

Ryerson couldn't resist. "I know the song. I'll sing it with you. Get on your horse."

Moon Dog stepped to the horse and made a grab for the saddle horn. As he did, he looked into Ryerson's eyes as though seeking something. Ryerson couldn't be certain, but he sensed he caught a flicker of growing doubt in the Indian's dark, flinty eyes. Ryerson had carried both Winchesters on their march up the hill. He took a moment to ram Moon Dog's ineffective weapon into its under-stirrup boot.

With Moon Dog mounted, Bonner tagged behind on a long tether Ryerson had tied to the killer's secure hands. Bonner plodded with a stoic resignation Ryerson might have expected from some half-wit like Myles Antrim. Ryerson figured all the beating about the head Bonner had taken this day had turned him meek. With himself and Bonner afoot and Moon Dog in the saddle, the curious little company started up the ribbon of stage road in the direction of the station.

They talked little, only stubbornly putting one foot ahead of the other, watching the coming hills, grateful when they reached the top. Halfway down the other side, though, Ryerson realized it only meant there would be another hill to climb.

Bonner, staring straight ahead toward what he obviously thought was his approaching death, trudged dumbly alongside Moon Dog's horse, which the Indian kept at a slow walk, the rope to Bonner's hands trailing in the dust.

Ryerson's waist was now encircled again with his own Navy and with Pat Graydon's six-gun rig, the backstrap of Pat's handgun jutting backward at his left side. He felt he had plenty of firepower if the Antrims sent out a welcoming committee. Still, it was a long way to the stage station, and he had a strong hunch that the Antrims—having sent Moon Dog out to find him—would be content with making their stand there.

Climbing the fifth or sixth hill—Ryerson lost track—since they left Moon Dog's ambush site, he felt the dragging weight of his legs as he labored up the steeps. He realized how much the manhunt to bring in Cass and Bonner had taken out of him. Mere breathing was difficult and painful. His pulse beat like tiny hammers against his temples and in the cords and muscles of his neck and shoulders. His mouth and throat had dried to rawhide and tasted sour.

Walking was a struggle in itself, not to mention what it took to stay alert and keep track of his prisoners. The knowledge of the hostility, and the futility, of all this was strong in him.

Bonner, despite his resigned silence, would try another escape the first opening he got. The Indian on horseback had sworn revenge on Ryerson and would watch for any weakness or opening.

A hell of a note, Ryerson thought as he stumped

RYERSON'S MANHUNT

along, fighting a grinding weariness, battling for stamina, watching Moon Dog from the rear. Moon Dog stared straight ahead, keeping the horse at a slow walk, following the pace set by Bonner plodding in the dirt beside him.

The only sound was the measured plop of the horse's hooves; in the silence that surrounded them, the dull pounding rang ominously in Ryerson's ears; each thud—like the measured cadence of a clock pendulum—brought him closer to the showdown.

Ryerson watched the horse's head bob in annoying rhythm with its relaxed gait. He knew that Moon Dog could be expected to move the moment his guard was down, and he was exhausted, the fatigue dulling his alertness as they slid down another grade and began to slow the pace, setting their feet aginst the slope of the next hill. Ryerson knew that Moon Dog's mind was not as empty as his slouch in the saddle would indicate. His mind, experienced in Apache cunning, was at work, planning each move and what he would do to wreak his vengeance in the event this, that, or something else happened. Ryerson calculated that already Moon Dog had a half-dozen plots hatched in his head.

Moon Dog had lived five years with the passion for revenge, only to have fate dump his target practically in his lap. Ryerson studied the Indian again; five years was a long time to live with the bitterness of hate, particularly Indian versus white man.

Ryerson shook his head at the utter futility of his quest. A lesser man would drill both of them here and now, take the horse and vamoose. It was an easy, appealing notion in his weary mind, and with a body that shouted at him to flee the situation any way he could and get off somewhere warm and soft and sleep—sleep maybe for days.

Ryerson's head and eyes snapped alert. There was still honor to deal with.

And Kate Folsom.

Ryerson knew he was not a lesser man; it was built in—at the Battle of Helena, Arkansas, and Captain Dan Sturgis taking the mortal thrust of a Yankee saber intended for him instead, and a great many other noble deaths of soldiers and lawmen he had lived with and fought beside, men he admired and respected, up to and including Sheriff Pat Graydon. No, there'd be no shirking responsibility. These honored dead shall not have died in vain. In vision, he saw the rock cairn in a forlorn grove on the prairie way off there someplace, and remembered his vow to the dead Pat Graydon. But there was more to it, even than that—those men who had helped mold his life before losing theirs.

He'd been a challenge to himself, too, dammit, he thought, trudging along the desolate road behind the Indian's horse. He'd lived his life seeking what in his own mind was right and just and giving it both barrels. Somehow, he knew, he could cope with Bonner and Moon Dog. He had them at bay, weaponless; both knew enough of the situation that any threatening moves would at least bring them a bullet that would wound. Everything, out here at least, worked in his favor. Bonner was dulled by the pain in his head; he wouldn't try anything. With his game leg, Moon Dog couldn't move fast either.

The real threat, the true question mark, lay ahead; the Antrims. As he walked, Ryerson tried to set aside the dragging fatigue by concentrating on the Antrims and how he would handle them when all this came to a head in a few hours. The three brothers were forted up with their prisoners in a stage station cabin. With Kate Folsom and the five people from the stage, the Antrims had him in a death grip and were beginning to squeeze.

It would be futile to go in and try to talk with Mitch. They'd get the drop on him some way, and Bonner's hash would be settled—and possibly his own as well, for getting in their way. Maybe he could coax Mitch out into the open to negotiate. This would be his only chance; appeal to Mitch's reason. Huh! he thought; that's no good. They had killed Cass and by now they knew that they, too, had a price on their heads.

Huh! Ryerson nearly grunted aloud. The deck was surely stacked against him. If it wasn't, at least he had a bum hand and his entire roll was in the pot. Somebody else had the power in this game.

A shrewd poker player, about now, would fold his hand, drop out and wait for a better deal, or leave the table for the night. If only it were that simple, Ryerson thought. But this was no simple card game he could back out of. In effect, he was in to the last call, betting his life on the next turn of the cards.

In a poker game, Ryerson mused, his steps slowing as he attacked another slope in the road, there would be only one thing to do now—set a poker face and pull off a good bluff. Play 'em as though you had 'em.

Pretend you've got the power. Hell, he thought, finding new resolve in his thoughts, I've got the power. My word, my will, against theirs. They're in the wrong, all of them, and they know it. That gives me the power hand. They're all bullies; cowards at heart. Maybe except for Moon Dog; he's a good man misguided. He's the one I've somehow got to make my ally. The others will be easy to bluff.

Once that course was reasonably firm in his mind, the old sense of power and command flowed back. The next slope, no worse nor better than the ones before, became easier. Ryerson began to look forward to the challenge of backing down the Antrims and rescuing Kate safely and bringing Bonner to justice. He would forget Moon Dog's attempt on his life. He strode up alongside the Indian's horse.

"Come on, Bonner," he shouted, almost cheerily.

"Shake a leg. The rate you're going, we won't get there before breakfast tomorrow morning."

Beside him, Moon Dog's voice was a bass mutter. "Not long now, anyway. We will see my place in daylight."

Ryerson looked to the west at the waning sun. It would be dark in an hour.

⇒ 21 ⇐

Moon Dog was right. Ryerson saw the stage station in daylight.

Already it cast a square clot of darkening shadow on its east side, irregularly edged where it lay over rutted, uneven ground.

The frame cabin looked innocent enough as it huddled there, though the abrupt sight of the place caused a catch of apprehension as the three of them crested the final hill and looked down on it. He felt his throat tighten in anxiety for what the next few moments and hours would bring. His leg muscles trembled from the long effort of the hike in, and a profound weariness had come over him. He was in no shape to face the challenge that was sure to come, vicious, ugly, and final.

He had come, at last, to the final showdown.

"Hold it right here," he called softly, and Moon Dog reined his horse to a halt and sat stoically. Bonner abruptly dropped to his butt in the dirt and crossed his legs, Indian style. His head hung in fatigue and he rested his roped hands on his knees.

The stage road they had followed through the grass dipped to the cabin. A great circle of terra-cotta earth packed hard as a slab of rock showed where stages had parked and circled, and where people had walked and horses had been changed.

The cabin was large enough to accommodate a number of people during stage stopovers, though in its squatness, it seemed to hug the land. Away from the worn circle in front, the road picked up again and meandered away to the northwest on its route to Medicine Springs.

Beside the cabin a large pole corral held a good-sized remuda—the Antrims' replacement horses and those Ryerson had left with Kate. Ryerson also saw four from the team that had hauled in the stage and four left in Moon Dog's care for stage replacements. He also identified the Folsoms' two workhorses. The story of this manhunt, Ryerson thought, was pretty well told in the collection in the corral.

The empty stagecoach stood beside the corral, its long tongue resting in the dust. The harness was haphazardly looped over the corral fence.

On the grassy slope some distance from the cabin and low-slung barn, two milk cows grazed, lending an almost pastoral atmosphere to the otherwise desolate scene. The cows were doubtlessly kept for milk for the stage passengers' meals.

Beside the barn and tack building, a dense stand of trees showed where a spring probably bubbled forth eternally—one reason for building the stage stop here. Near the grove perched a small outhouse, maybe a two-holer, its door closed.

As the three paused on the slope to the south, a man left the outhouse and trudged, head down, toward the cabin, carrying a shotgun. From the absent, splay-footed walk of the man, Ryerson recognized Myles Antrim.

Myles was halfway to the cabin when his head came up and he spotted the two men afoot and one on horseback on the knoll overlooking the cabin.

Myles burst into his half-wit stumbling, shuffling run and disappeared into the cabin's back door. Even at the distance, Ryerson could hear the thud of the heavy door as Myles closed it. He was aware of his quickened heartbeat; in a moment Mitch and Mort would know he had arrived with Bonner. The fat was in the fire and beginning to smoke.

"All right, Moon Dog," he commanded softly. "Leave your horse here and go down on foot."

Without a word Moon Dog hoisted his game leg out of the stirrup and over his saddle and slid to the ground with an awkward bounce, skipping once to catch his balance. "It's your play, Ryerson," he growled.

"Tell Mitch he has two choices. He can come out, unarmed, to meet me to talk. Or, if he won't hear it from me, my orders are to release Mrs. Folsom and the people from the stage. Then he and his brothers can turn themselves over to me peaceably and go into Patchknife to be charged with the murder of Sam Cass."

Moon Dog reacted with shock and rage. "You're out of your mind! You don't expect me to—"

"Of course I expect you to. They sent you out to bring me in, and here I am and that is what you are to tell them."

"And if I refuse?"

"When this is all over, I'll take you with them to stand trial for attempted murder. Of me. Cooperate and I'll forget what happened out there and merely assume you were a little trigger-happy."

"You aren't getting out of this alive, Ryerson. If they don't get you, I will."

"Are you willing to bet a charge of attempted murder against that? You already tried once and failed. How much more fooling around do you plan to do? Defy me and I'll also nail you for obstructing justice.

You may be well-liked in these parts, pardner, but you're still an Indian. Old hatreds die hard."

"I'll get a gun and fight you side by side with them."

"That's a choice I can't make for you. I've already made it clear where I stand on your actions from this point."

"I'll go in and tell Mitch Antrim. He'll probably gun me down on the spot."

"I'm thinking he won't. You're only doing what he told you to do. It will be dark soon. I want to hear something from Mitch before night. Tell him to come out unarmed with his hands up. But tell him I'll come with my rifle. I won't chance his brothers bushwhacking me."

"He'll never agree to that, and you know it, Ryerson."

"Those are my terms. Tell him he has no other choice."

"I'm telling you he'll kill all of us in there."

"And I remember that you hid out there and nearly emptied your Winchester at me. You don't have any choices in the matter, either. Cut the palaver and get down there and deliver my message."

For a long moment Moon Dog's eyes probed deep into Ryerson's as they stood scant inches from each other. The Indian appeared to be searching in his mind for some other way to solve Ryerson's problem, save his own life, and appease the Antrims. Abruptly Moon Dog did an almost military about-face and stumped toward the cabin, his crippled leg thumping like a log against the earth.

Going down the steep, grassy slope of hill toward the flats around the cabin, Moon Dog hopped on his good leg as he picked up speed on the grade. Once on the grassless expanse twenty-five yards from the cabin, he called out:

"Antrim! It's me. Moon Dog. Don't shoot!"

Ryerson heard a muffled response from inside the

cabin and the door swung open a crack. In the gathering darkness around and behind the crack, Ryerson caught sight of part of a face peering out and a Winchester leveled in the doorway. Moon Dog shoved the door wide open and limped inside; it shut with another thud.

"All right, Bonner," Ryerson said. "Now to get you settled until this is over."

"For God's sake, Ryerson, whatcha gonna do?"

"I'm afraid I'm going to have to take you back out of the way and hog-tie you. I may have my hands full protecting myself here before long. I won't need to be worrying about you."

"Aw, Ryerson, give me a fighting chance, will ya? When they get you, I'll be a sittin' duck."

"Look, Bonner, I don't have time for fool arguments from you. You ain't exactly been a model prisoner, you know! Now don't get muley or I'll put you to sleep again. You know damned well I can do it."

There seemed little argument left in Lacey Bonner. He had failed in two escape tries and both times got hurt for it. He appeared reluctant now to keep bucking Ryerson's will, knowing the next time he might fail for good and all.

Ryerson untied Bonner's tether rope from Moon Dog's saddle and led him and the horse back down off the bluff behind them. "Come on now, fast. I've got to get busy and get this mess settled in that cabin and get you safely to Patchknife." He spoke more to himself than to Bonner. "Get down on your belly."

Bonner meekly obeyed, taking the position. Ryerson untied one of Bonner's hands and retied them together behind his back. He threw a loop of rope around Bonner's booted ankles, bent his knees back and snubbed the rope securely to Bonner's wrists. Without more argument, the big man settled in to the uncomfortable position on his side, rested his head on the ground and closed his eyes.

With Bonner secured, Ryerson again led the horse back to the knoll above the cabin site. Nothing had happened while he'd been gone. The yard was empty except for the more than a dozen horses milling in the corral.

Ryerson perched on the hilltop, holding the horse's reins in plain sight of the cabin. It had one window, and in the gathering dusk he saw that it was curtained. As he watched, the curtain fluttered as someone lifted it partially to look out at him. The distance was too great and dusk too deep for much of a rifle shot. Ryerson stayed calm, knowing he was on reasonably safe ground.

Besides, he thought, a show of guts maybe was what was needed along about now. A good strong bluff, what he had planned all along, required a hefty dose of heroics; maybe an almost foolhardy portion. In spite of his tensions, he grinned; that was the name of this whole damned, dumb game—foolhardy.

Fortune favors fools, he was once told. Fools with guts, maybe, he thought. And that was the impression he wanted to give that bunch in the cabin. That's what the man, whoever he was, peeking under the curtain, was seeing.

To the west the sun had already bid the world good night. It would not be pitch-dark for another twenty minutes. Already the land had begun to cool after the hot afternoon and early evening; a soft, pleasant feel filled the air around him, comforting and easing him. He'd staved off his physical exhaustion now for hours, and the approach of cool night seemed to bolster him. He was ready to take on what was to come. His stomach nagged at him as the supper hour neared, but he knew it might yet be some hours before he'd be in a position for a good meal. They were no doubt eating inside—probably forcing Kate to prepare the meal.

His mind turned on Kate, hoping they hadn't mistreated her. If they had, he didn't know at this point if he could hold back his fury. While he sat there, his mind on her, the cabin door opened, stabbing him with a new jolt of alarm. Tom Moon Dog came out quickly and in his stumbling limp, as though he'd been rudely shoved. There was still enough light to see he had his arms over his head to show he wasn't armed as he made his way across the beaten, flat earth and started up the hill where Ryerson waited.

Moon Dog labored as he made his way up the grassy knoll. He walked ramrod stiff with anger and emotion. "May your white man's God damn you, Ryerson. I told you it wouldn't work."

"What did Mitch say?"

"What I told you he'd say. No deals. Only now it is worse. You have until sunup to turn Bonner over to them. Why is that man's life worth so much to you?"

"He doesn't mean a thing."

"Then give him to them."

"It's principle, Tom. I hoped by now you'd understand." It was the first time he'd called the Apache by his first name. Moon Dog seemed to take no note of it. "What about the woman? How is she?"

"She is very tired. The Antrims tell her that Ryerson values Bonner's life more than hers. She does not listen. But she is very tired."

"What's Mitch's deal?"

"I told you. No deal. Give them Bonner now and ride on."

"He knows I'm taking him to Patchknife."

"Mitch says you'd better not ride on with Bonner. He wants him."

"And if I take him?"

"He'll kill everybody in there, Mrs. Folsom and me right along with them, and then he'll ride you down. You only have my horse there. You and Bonner are as good as dead if you leave."

"So that's it."

"No, that's not it. Let me go back, Ryerson, and

tell them now that they can have Bonner. That's all. He gives you till sunup. First light. That's when the killing starts. One of us—and Mitch hasn't yet decided—gets shoved out into the yard and gunned down in your plain sight."

"Of all the low, son of a bitching—"

"Every hour you delay, one more person dies the same way."

"Mitch will just pound nails into his own coffin."

Moon Dog's voice rose. "Then you go down and tell him that, Boot Hill Cole. You've got to give in to him. The blood of those people will be on your hands. Even white man's law won't allow you to keep Bonner away from them while seven innocent people die. That goes against your 'principle,' white man!"

"They won't die, Tom." In the deepening dark, Ryerson hoped Moon Dog would see his grin. "We're not going to let them kill those people."

"We?"

"Yeah. You and me."

22

"You can't stay out here too long, Tom. They'll think we're plotting."

"They've no reason to fear. I won't take your side, Ryerson. I've told you that. They know it. They know I tried to kill you. And why."

"I hope Mitch finds strength in that thought. He's going to need it. Still, in spite of what you know of them, you'll desert me? They're murderers, Tom. Evil. Like Major Lemuel Hardcastle. Can you honestly take the side of men like that against me because of some hearsay that I was the one who crippled you?"

"Five years of being worthless as a man is a long time. We were once sworn enemies, you and me. Still are."

Ryerson grunted. "Yeah, I suppose you've every right to your bitterness, Tom. If I were in your shoes, I'm sure I'd be as bitter as you. After the five years you've carried it around inside, it would be impossible for me, at least now, to persuade you that I was not the man who crippled you. I was there, but I assure you it was not me."

"You fired the bullet into my leg. I did not see you. Others in my village saw you there and saw you shoot me from behind. Ryerson, the marshal from Fort Walker, was well-known to us."

"Under the circumstances, Tom, anything I say sounds like a desperate man lying to save his skin. But I do not lie. A while ago today we spoke of living with lies. Tom, hear well; I do not live with one!"

"So. You have Mitch Antrim's message. My part in this is finished."

"Except that you will be accessory to murder. Wait, Tom. Have you heard that a man cannot lie and look you in the eye at the same time?"

"All white men lie. And with a straight face."

"What does it take to convince you? All I ask is try it with me. Come closer. It's nearly dark. I want you to be able to see my eyes clearly."

Moon Dog edged closer. His eyes searched Ryerson's again. The eyes Ryerson watched seemed less flinty than earlier in the day. The look in them said that Moon Dog wanted to believe, even if his mouth couldn't find the words. Ryerson only hoped he wasn't reading Moon Dog's eyes wrong.

Ryerson stared hard into Moon Dog's eyes. "In my heart, Tom, I know I was not the one who gunned you down. My assignment from Judge Winfield at Fort Walker was to serve with the scout contingent against Little Pete's forces. Hardcastle's invasion of Mexico was totally contrary to orders. I was obliged to take part even though it was contrary to my instructions from Judge Winfield, and I told you I did make a full report to him at Fort Walker. However, to Hardcastle, I had reported finding your village, and personally told Hardcastle that the camp was mostly women, children, and old men, and only a handful of Apache warriors. You must have been one of them."

Moon Dog's eyes acknowledged what Ryerson had said. His eyes were close to Ryerson's and unblinking, though they moved ever so slightly as they searched for a flicker of deceit.

"When Hardcastle ordered the attack, I advised strongly against it. We had come in at great risk to engage Little Pete's warriors and try to effect a capture and return them to the territories. I knew an attack on this village was totally inhuman and wrong. Furthermore, it would alert Little Pete and he would vanish into the mountains and become even more bitter and hostile—which, as you know, is exactly what happened."

Ryerson continued to bore his unwavering stare into Moon Dog's eyes.

"Against my will, I was ordered—at the risk of being shot as a deserter—to ride with Hardcastle. Now look at me close. I had no power to stop the attack. So I rode with the man. But I swear to you, Tom Moon Dog, my rifle stayed in the boot. I fired only my Navy revolver—this one right here—and then only for effect. I made certain that not a single round from my weapon harmed an Apache. You have no cause to believe me, but in my heart, I know I could not be the man who crippled you."

With the last of his words, Ryerson looked into eyes rimmed with moisture. It could only have been the emotion of recalling the battle and seeing his people massacred and himself taking a crippling wound.

Still, Ryerson hadn't expected Moon Dog's reaction.

"You will have to fight your own battles and handle this situation the best way you can, Ryerson," he said. Again Moon Dog about-faced and disappeared into the dark down the hill. Ryerson quickly lost sight of him, but heard his distinctive footsteps grow dimmer as he struggled down the road to the cabin.

As the quiet returned to the land around him, Ryerson cursed his inability to reach Moon Dog with logic; the Indian had been his only possible ally. Indeed, he would have to handle the situation as he'd done most everything in life—by himself. Alone, totally alone, against overwhelming odds, he must think it through.

Plan a course to save his own hide, on the line now as never before, without help from any quarter. Kate would be strong and willing, but under the circumstances, with absolutely no means of communication, undependable. Ryerson studied the sky, one or two distant planets emerging as tiny, sparkling golden orbs of light. He had six, at the most seven, hours to work out a strategy.

Sleep this night is out of the question, he told himself, though his fatigue lay like a heavy load inside him, his mind dim with the burden of it. He could rest his body, but not his mind nor his eyes. Still, he determined to maintain his vigil on the cabin. In these final hours he must decide how, singlehandedly, he would thwart the Antrims and prevent their mass slaughter of the hostages. Ryerson had no delusions that Mitch Antrim didn't mean business with his threat; he was up against desperate men who had already murdered in their drive to see an end to their vengeance, despite the cost in human life.

Ryerson studied the burgeoning stars, feeling greater frustration, now that his revelations had had no effect on Moon Dog. Obviously the reaction was negative or the Indian would have stayed to plot how they would work together to solve the thorny problem.

Overhead the stars had come up in sheer grandeur; the Big Dipper's great arched handle and three-sided rectangle were clearly outlined against the velvet blackness. Around it, above and below it, the great ebony dome over him sparkled and gleamed with pinpoints of yellow light on the dusty golden background of much farther constellations and stars.

Out like this under less trying circumstances, Ryerson would marvel at the heavens at night, enjoying and reveling in the awesome depths revealed by the dark sky, as much as he appreciated the beauty of the land by day. But this was no time for rejoicing in the depths of the night sky. He knew that in a number of hours, the Antrims threatened the wholesale butchering of seven human beings.

Ryerson pondered it for the hundredth time. He could not, would not, turn Bonner over to them. he had to stop them before daylight, or at least before they murdered their first victim. In spite of his need for realism, he fantasized a grand dramatic play of sneaking to the side of the cabin in the dark and, as the first victim was shoved out, bolting through the door, two guns blazing, hoping to hit Antrims and not the innocents.

He came out of the reverie abruptly, shaking himself alert and damning himself for allowing such futile mind-play when he needed serious concentration on his dilemma. He was also aware that his desperate need for sleep had prompted the illusion. He must concentrate, he shouted inwardly; he must stay awake. Maybe, he thought, his mind alert again, there was some way to divide the Antrims and incapacitate them one by one without the others knowing it and prematurely starting the slaughter.

Maybe he'd start by taking Myles prisoner in the morning when he went out to the privy, and use him as a bargaining point. No, that assumed that Myles would come out before the killing started.

He thought of luring Mitch and Mort out, taking a chance on the two-to-one odds. Myles, without a doubt, would cave in and be ineffective as anything but a pawn, probably more of a liability. Mitch and Mort, really, were his primary adversaries. He'd somehow have to get to them. But now? They would be watching for a trick, and were not easily tricked. Ryerson grew furious with himself that he had come up with absolutely no plan that didn't involve a threat to the hostages. His mind felt strangled in its failure to come up with anything workable. He closed his eyes against staring at the cubed chunk of black cabin in the land before him and the sky full of stars towering over it, and fought in his head for solutions. At least he could rest his burning eyes for a moment; only for a minute or two.

In that minute, and for quite a few before that, Ryerson had forgotten Moon Dog's horse. Freed of the man's hold on the reins, the horse had slowly cropped its way off the knoll behind him, taking the line of least resistance as it grazed downhill in the tall grass, moving slowly. Its hooves made small sounds against the grass and earth as it moved, the only sound being the easy gnashing of its teeth against the tender spears of grass it nipped free.

In the swale below, the horse was suddenly brought alert by the writhing of a man in the grass. For hours Lacey Bonner had pitted his brute strength against the ropes that restrained his hands and kept his knees drawn up behind him in the painful hog-tied position. All his stubborn struggling had only served to pull the knots tighter, but his wrists were loose in the loops that held them.

Quivering with the intense effort, sweating profusely, Bonner stretched and pulled himself until, groping with frenzied fingers, he found the knot that held his feet drawn up into the middle of his back. Feverishly, cursing under his breath at the unyielding ropes, he worked and worried with feverish haste at the hitch that immobilized his legs. His sweat-slick fingers plucked at the knots, accomplishing little. Then, by degrees, the rope slipped in its knots, the binding began to loosen, and immediately and almost miraculously, the bonds gave and his feet and legs were free.

Bonner bounced erect, spurred by his newfound freedom, looking around him in the dark for a sign of Ryerson, flexing his stiff legs against the cramp of the uncomfortable hours on the cold ground. Nearby, an outcropping of rock showed a short chisel edge.

Bonner backed up to it and began to saw at his wrist ropes. As he did, the sharp edge chewed skin and flesh from the insides of his wrists and he could feel the salt sting as grit ground into raw, bleeding flesh. Still, he fought like a man possessed at cutting through the ropes.

At last these, too, gave way, and suddenly he was free, shaking his arms to rid them of the numbing paralysis of confinement and the pain and smarting of his torn, aching wrists. The severed ropes dropped away.

Quietly he edged to the grazing horse, a familiar dark shape against the silent blackness, taking care not to panic the animal. He grabbed the reins, hurled himself into the saddle and headed the horse for the southbound stage road, the way he had come only hours before.

In his deep, involuntary sleep, Ryerson did not miss the horse, and did not hear the racing hoofbeats on the packed dirt of the road behind him. As Lacey Bonner began his desperate flight for freedom, Ryerson continued to sleep, drugged by his hours of physical fatigue and emotional strain.

Ryerson first became aware of something cold and round shoved against his cheek, and a gruff voice commanding him. It took him a while to realize that the coldness was a round gun muzzle.

"All right, Ryerson! On your feet!" It seemed to take forever for his dulled brain to respond. He lay there, slowly coming awake. He yearned to be left alone to continue his blessed slumbers.

The two bulking angrily over him in the dark had to be Mort and Myles Antrim. Ryerson sat bolt upright in sudden realization.

"We got 'im, Mort!" Myles enthused. Ryerson heard the words as from a long distance as his brain still fought its way slowly back to reality.

"Get up, Ryerson, and don't go for them guns!" Mort backed away, holding the rifle on him as Ryerson got to his feet. "Drop the belts. Myles, get that Winchester there. You been wantin' a nice rifle, so there y'are."

Ryerson saw no point in resisting. Mort Antrim meant business, his big hulk towering in the dark beside Ryerson. In these early morning hours, the land had turned cold. Ryerson trembled against it.

"I'll guard this one, Myles. You go see if you can find that big fella we're lookin' for. He's around somewhere tied up, I allow."

"Hee hee," Myles cackled. "Now maybe we gonna git to hang that 'un up an' built a fa'r under his head like we done that other 'un, Mort!"

"Yeah, Myles," Mort reassured. "And Mitch says you can do it with this here Ryerson, too."

Myles looked at Ryerson like a hungry man leering at a fat pig he was about to butcher. Still cackling, Myles stumped off into the dark, beating about in the night looking for Bonner.

Ryerson was fully alert. "Well, Antrim, how'd you do it? I know I was sleeping. But what made you sneak up here?"

"Not harm tellin' now. That Injun."

Ryerson was shot through with rage; Moon Dog surely had pulled out all the stops in aligning himself with the Antrims. "Damn him," Ryerson muttered.

"He wouldn't tell us what you fellas talked about up here. So Mitch had Myles go to work on that bum leg of his. He told us everything we wanted to know. He ain't much of an Apache. Myles give one good twist on that leg of his and he opened up like a gutted possum. We figured you for bein' plumb tuckered, so me and Myles done what you done to us the other night. Only this time we're gonna take more than your horse and your boots."

It seemed a long time before Myles was back, an

apologetic whine in his voice. "I can't find 'im nowheres, Mort." Myles seemed on the verge of tears.

"All right, Ryerson," Mort demanded. "Where you got Bonner hid? The Injun told us he was up here somewheres with you."

Aware that Bonner had probably made good his escape, Ryerson turned arrogant. Might as well, he thought; nothing to lose now. He had also turned bold knowing Moon Dog's resistance only thawed under the agony of torture. "I guess that's for me to know and for you to find out, Antrim," he said.

"I'd ought to whop you one right in that big mouth of yours, Ryerson. But all right. Yours is comin' anyway. Bonner's got to be around here someplace, or not far off. Hustle this one down to the cabin, Myles, and let's see what Mitch has to say about all this."

23

Myles had lumbered ahead to the cabin with the good tidings and the bad; they had captured Ryerson, but Bonner had gotten away. As Mitch rudely shoved Ryerson through the open door with the light streaming from inside, Mitch Antrim's bulking silhouette filled the entry, blocking much of the light. Ryerson stumbled in ahead of Mort, who kept a Winchester leveled at the small of Ryerson's back. There was challenge in Mitch's stance as he blocked Ryerson's way.

"What'd you do with him, outlander?" Mitch demanded. "You let 'im go, didn't ya?"

As he neared Mitch, Ryerson's nose was assaulted by a rancid, repulsive breath and body smell. Mitch hadn't bathed recently but he sure had been drinking. Angrily, Mitch cocked his right arm to take a poke at Ryerson's head. Ryerson ducked and the swing went wild. The butt of Mort's rifle dealt Ryerson a mean blow in the small of his back and he pitched forward to bowl over Mitch; the two landed in a heap inside the cabin.

Mitch jumped up and brutally hoisted the limp lawman to his feet by the back of his coat. Ryerson's body ached, the pain rolling into his legs, which threatened to buckle.

"Wha'd ya do that for, Mort?" Mitch demanded.

" 'Cause he needed it," Mort responded.

Ryerson's eyes, dimmed by the pain and his fatigue, sought to identify the brightly lit room and the people in it. A handful of men—his numbed brain didn't register how many—sat anxiously at a large and long table in the good-sized room. At one side of the room was a bar for serving drinks as well as food to stage travelers stopping over. The faces Ryerson saw at the table were gray with the strain. Kate Folsom, looking small and alone, sat at one end of the table. She looked haggard as she watched Ryerson intently, afraid to make any move in his direction, though her expression said she wanted to. Their eyes met and Kate nodded imperceptibly.

Ryerson didn't see Moon Dog. Enclosed, criblike rooms appeared to line the walls, and Ryerson surmised one was Moon Dog's sleeping room and that he was probably there, nursing his aching crippled leg, which had been worked over by the Antrims. His eyes returned to Kate's, and he nodded back, trying with his eyes to reassure her, but not wanting the Antrims to see any signal pass between them.

"Where is he, Ryerson?" Mitch demanded. "What'd you do with him?"

Ryerson laid heavy on the truth. "I left Bonner hogtied out in the grass. Behind where Mort and Myles found me. It's evident that since Myles didn't find him back there, he somehow got himself loose and is on his way out of these parts on Moon Dog's horse."

He tried to assure himself that maybe the worst was over. Maybe now the Antrims would let them all go in their haste to get back to Bonner's trail.

"Yeah," Mort said from behind Ryerson. "And we got to go get him. Whataya think, Mitch?"

"Gimme a minute to think, gawdammit! How long ago did he leave, outlander?"

"I have no idea."

"You lyin' son of a bitch!" Mitch screamed. With the flat of his hand he swung out and slapped Ryerson hard enough across the cheek to knock him off balance again, stinging his face from the blow and sending a jarring fog into his head. Ryerson reeled slightly, caught himself and quickly regained his defiant position in front of Mitch. He decided the last thing in the world he would do was cower before these bullies.

"Myles!" Mitch snapped. "Take a lamp and get out there fast and saddle up Nick and Jenny. They're the two fastest we got."

Myles stared at Mitch, his tongue making its circuit around his lips.

"Judas!" Mitch roared. "Now, gawdammit, Myles!"

Myles grabbed a lamp near him and scooted out the door.

"Mort, you and Myles go after that son of a bitch Bonner. It'll be daylight in a little while. He couldn't have got far. He'd be slow in the dark. I want that bastard back here pronto."

"Can you hold all these folks alone, Mitch? 'Specially with this one around? Got to watch him. He's slick."

Mitch looked around him with a self-satisfied smirk. "You go do what you got to do and let me worry about the outlander, and you see what a pushover he is. These other birds won't try nothing funny. We got the redskin laid up good and proper for at least a couple a days. They start makin' any wrong moves and I'll take half the room with Myles's scattergun. Don't worry about that, Mort. Now what in the everlastin' hell is takin' your lamebrained brother so long? Go hurry him up, Mort, and get crackin'." Mort darted out of the cabin.

From outside, Ryerson heard some high-pitched argumentative words, then the same voices urging the horses. There were tentative thumps of hooves outside the corral and two horses broke into a gallop, the sound rapidly fading as Mort and Myles tore at a fast clip up the hill and out the south road. Ryerson stood where he had been, a few steps inside the door.

"Make yourselves comfortable, gents," Mitch announced happily to the fearful-looking group of stage passengers. "Catch a few winks of shut-eye if you want to. When my brothers get back with the man they went after, we'll put you back on the stage first thing and you can be on your way, no hard feelings."

The stage passengers and the driver stayed nervously at the table. It was evident from their tight, pale expressions that they had been through an ordeal. At Mitch's words, none of them moved or spoke.

"What do you want me to do?" Ryerson asked.

Mitch glared at him as he waved the shotgun barrels in his direction. "Well, sit down, for crissakes. Looks like since your friend Bonner got away from you, you earned a few more hours to live till they get back here with him. Long as you behave yourself, that is. You're a pretty sly customer, Ryerson, so you mind your p's and q's. Go sit with your lady friend there. Hear tell you two done a sight of travelin' together."

Ryerson started toward the table where Kate sat watching him. His body still hurt, but he was recovering quickly. He stopped. "Mitch, don't make all this harder on yourself. You and your brothers have already murdered one man—"

"Aw, shut the hell up!" Mitch roared savagely. "Go sit down with the lady there and quit giving me that preacher-pulpit bullshit!"

"Is it proper to ask if I can go ahead and talk to her?"

"Sure, for crissakes. Talk's cheap these days. I ain't stoppin' ya, am I? Go to billin' and cooin' for all I care. Mind you don't go pullin' any fast ones. From here I can sling enough buckshot to paint you all over that wall yonder."

Ryerson eyed the cannonlike muzzles of the sawed-off twelve-gauge with respect. Mitch could and would do it.

Ryerson scraped up a vacant chair to where Kate sat at the table. As he sat down, he eyed Mitch again. Antrim's eyes were bright and alert as a squirrel's. Though Ryerson had no idea when Mitch had slept last, he could see that the job of command and being close to having Bonner in his clutches had him thoroughly nerved up. There wasn't a chance in a million that Mitch would doze, as he himself had up on the hill. He cursed himself for falling asleep. He shivered. That brief nap might mean the closing of his eyes for good and all.

Still, he had to figure how he could get in under those scattergun barrels in what little time he had before Mort and Myles got back with Bonner—and he was convinced they would. Mitch would be furious and rattle-brained enough to kill them all if his brothers returned empty-handed.

They were certain to get back before long. Bonner couldn't have had that much of a head start. Ryerson pulled his chair close enough to touch Kate, to be able to talk so everyone in the room didn't have to hear. "You all right, Kate?"

She looked ten years older in the almost three days since he'd seen her. Her eyes, the ones he remembered as bright and flashing, were listless, dark orbs in sunken, gray pockets. Her cheeks were shriveled, and the flaming and vibrant copper hair he had admired hung dull and lifeless around her neck and shoulders. Even the hand she reached over and tenderly rested on his felt cold and waxy. "I knew you'd come for me, Cole. I knew you wouldn't leave me for those maniacs to kill."

"You fellas play some cards or something, if you

wanna," Mitch called to the men in the room. They looked quizzically and then went back to staring blankly ahead. They were mostly old men, Ryerson noted; probably too old to enjoy going horseback any more and probably went by stage when they had to go somewhere.

Mitch got up, went to the bar and grabbed a half-filled bottle off the top. On his way back to the chair, he worked the cork free and had a long pull before he sat down.

Maybe that's my opening, Ryerson thought. If he gets to drinking heavily, his reaction time may slow enough that I can try to take him. Still, he reasoned, Mitch was a heavy drinker who probably could put away a barrelful and not be fazed.

"I shouldn't have let you come along, Kate. It was wrong from the start."

"Don't punish yourself, Cole. Things didn't work out the way we thought."

"It was good for a while, wasn't it, Kate? The day before we caught up with them." Ryerson saw some of the old brightness come up in her eyes with the remembering.

"We almost made it, didn't we, Cole?" Her hand squeezed his under the table. When she spoke again, it was with a definite tremor. "They're going to kill us, aren't they Cole?"

Ryerson tried to sound reassuring. "They want Bonner. I don't know."

"They will. For interfering. I know they will. I was there when Cass . . ." Ryerson felt a convulsive shiver rack Kate's body.

"Don't talk about it, Kate. Don't remember it."

"You're such a good man, Cole Ryerson. I've got to say this while I still have time. You are so good . . ." Her voice lowered to a soft and hoarse whisper. ". . . and they are so goddamned evil!"

"I know," he said, lowering his voice, too. "And

always being right and just doesn't mean that you'll always come out on top. I guess I should have given them Bonner when I had the chance, and hoped the evidence would clear me of negligence. Because of my bullheadedness about that, these people—"

"No, Cole, no, you couldn't have turned Bonner over for them to murder, no matter what happens now. You'd hate yourself the rest of your life and carry an awful burden on your shoulders. No, for a man like you, dying would be easier. I know you that well, Cole Ryerson."

He put his other hand on top of hers. "At least somebody does, Kate. I love you for that."

Kate's word rang with an even deeper meaning. "And I love you, Cole. I've never really loved before, even though I was married all those years. I know that now. I think I started loving you that day at the cabin. You had so many things on your mind, urgent things, but you put them aside in your concern for me, with Leander stretched out there, him dead only a few hours and all."

"I've loved you, too, Kate ... since then."

Her voice turned low again. "I'd kiss you, but I don't think all these people would understand. They know I'm lately a widow."

"Particularly Mitch Antrim."

Kate's smile was genuine. "At least he'd have something to say about it."

"What about Tom Moon Dog?"

"I don't think they broke his leg, but they made Myles twist it to make him tell what you two talked about so long up on the hill."

"Did he?"

"He was gone so long, they figured Moon Dog and you had to be in cahoots. When he wouldn't tell them anything, they were sure the two of you were up to something. Mort held him down, and Myles caught hold of his foot and twisted it. Tom took it a long time. It wasn't pretty. Tom has always been a good man, and I think he understood about Leander and the way he was. Like you. Considerate. And all the while, Tom didn't even scream. I don't think you'd scream, either."

"He's Apache. They learn early not to show weakness."

"But I could see that the pain was killing him. He finally told them that he had no use for you and told them about the raid that crippled his leg and that he held you responsible and tried to shoot and kill you."

"He did. He's a bum shot. It's all true, Kate. Except that I know I couldn't have been the one that wounded his leg. I tried to tell him that."

"That's when they let him up. He passed out, so they carried him to his room. Over there."

"I figured it. I suppose Moon Dog's bad enough hurt to be out of the action."

"What they did to his poor leg, even to a person with a good one, would lay a body up for a week."

"Damn! I thought he'd be smart enough to recognize the truth. With his help, we could have worked something out."

Through the curtained windows, Ryerson could see that daylight had come up fast. There were still a few options. It was a new day. He was in the cabin, and the Antrims' reasons for killing the stage riders one by one had passed. There was still hope.

He thought briefly of Moon Dog's sheath knife still jammed in his boot top. He might try hurling it at Antrim; if he missed, Mitch wouldn't hesitate in turning loose both shotgun barrels on the two of them.

All hope vanished as abruptly as the dark of night disappeared with the face of the sun stretching itself up out of bed to the east. In the hard-packed yard, Ryerson heard the furious galloping and reining up of three horses. Mort and Myles were back, and they had Bonner.

Inside the cabin, Ryerson was alerted to another sound. His head followed it. A door to one of the rooms had creaked slightly ajar; Tom Moon Dog stood behind the crack of opening, his face drawn and drained of color through his pain.

As quickly as Moon Dog saw Ryerson, Kate, and Mitch Antrim watching him, he backed up and closed the door.

≫ 24 ≪

Mort and Myles had taken the time, after catching up with Bonner and getting the drop on him, to work him over before bringing him in. One eye was blackening and his face was puffy and contused and turning a splotchy purple in places from their battering. His hands were again tied in front so he could handle a horse on the swift ride back to his fate.

Bonner's head hung and his eyes were downcast as Mort and Myles muscled him into the room. He came in defeated and slouching, to stand inside the door while Mitch got up to confront him.

"We—We got 'im, Mitch," Myles stammered. "Now do we—"

"He give us a bit of a time, Mitch," Mort interrupted. "We had to gentle him some. We knew we dasn't shoot him, so it was a job of work gettin' him bulldogged. Myles done most of it. You'd've been proud of our brother."

"Well," Mitch said, "you fellas sure as hell done yourselves proud. Hey! You-all from the stage. You're free to go now. The regular man, he ain't in much shape to harness up the team and get it in the traces. If some of you help, you can be on your way. Sorry for the delay, gents." And then aside, "Mort, sit that bastard Bonner down over there someplace till these folks get headed for home."

The stage passengers looked confusedly at each other. They scraped back their chairs and, still looking meekly at the Antrims as though they didn't believe their ears, picked up their belongings and filed out of the cabin. As long as Ryerson had been inside, he hadn't heard a peep out of any of them.

With their departure, he knew, also went any chance of organizing any resistance to the Antrims. That part was finished. Now he faced the three viciously determined brothers totally alone, with the added responsibility of Bonner, Kate Folsom, and probably Tom Moon Dog, incapacitated. Ryerson got up. Just now there seemed little to lose.

"Mitch," he began, and Mitch spun around angrily and impatiently. "That man there, Bonner, is my prisoner. I demand he be turned over to my custody to be properly tried and judged in Patchknife."

"Aw, hell, Ryerson. I told you to quit talkin' through your hat. He's due for a taste of western justice, all right. Not in Patchknife with a bunch of your pantywaist lawmen and judges. This shotgun is the law out here. You better mind your mouth or old Judge Buckshot'll find you in contempt of court." Mitch's face lit up and he cackled loudly over what he considered a meaningful and imaginative metaphor.

Ryerson was unmoved. "Pat Graydon deputized me the morning we started out after Cass and Bonner. Since Graydon is dead and there's no other deputy in this jurisdiction, that makes me sheriff and the law."

Mitch Antrim's face wrinkled in vile anger again. "On your say-so, which ain't worth a nickel that's been plugged by a .44. While you're talkin' about law, I say you broke the law in a big way the other night, you and your high-and-mighty sheriff. I'm talkin' about horse-thievin', mister, and stealin' a man's personal belongings, which don't go in this country."

Mort grinned smugly and stuck his face in close to Mitch and Ryerson. "And you know what we do with horse thieves in these parts?"

"Sure," Ryerson said, and he mustered the guts the mimic Myles. "You hang 'em up by they heels an' built a fa'r under they heads!" He returned to his regular voice. "Do that and the law will hound you all to your graves!"

"Well, damn you!" Mitch's eyes had tightened in a new, sudden anger. "I told you a long time back, mister, that this was an Antrim affair, but you had to go poking your outlander nose into it. I told you what would happen if you kept at it, and you did, and here you are. Now you're going to pay for it. You should've used your head six or seven days ago and hunted your hole like I told you, Ryerson. This here's Antrim business and we'll, by God, be gettin' on with it."

Ryerson continued defiantly. "You'll never make it, Mitch. Since you seem bound and determined to go through with this, at least have the human decency to let Mrs. Folsom get on a horse and get back to her ranch."

"She's in this as much as you."

Ryerson glanced at Kate, still seated at the table. Her face was tight and blanched in terror, her eyes wide with approaching hysteria. Mitch's voice again invaded a heavy silence.

"Mort, go on out and see if you can hurry those loafers along with that coach. Get 'em out of here so's we can 'tend to what has to be done here." Mitch disappeared into the bright sunlight outside.

When he left, Myles piped up. "Mitch, you mean now we gonna git to—"

Mitch was solicitous of his dimwit brother. "Yeah, Myles, you just be a good boy and wait a bit and you'll have your fun. Why don't you go over to my chair yonder and I'll tell you when we get started."

"Oh—Okay, Mitch. Okay." Myles stumped clumsily to the chair in the corner and sat down, a great, eager grin spread across his blank face. In anticipation, he licked his lips more frequently now.

Ryerson tried again. "Mitch, I have to protest this. Sometimes vigilante justice is called for when there's no adequate law around to look after the keeping of it. Believe me, I've risked plenty so far to get Bonner on his way to justice in Patchknife. Have no fear. I'll get him the rest of the way. You'll see justice done. I guarantee you."

"You won't quit, will you, outlander? You're forgettin', mister, that we already done half of what we set out for. When us Antrims set out to do a thing, it gets done."

"Then for crying out loud, at least do the merciful thing and let Mrs. Folsom go!"

Mitch forced a patient tone, almost as though he spoke to Myles. "Why don't you go back and set down next to the missus there and keep your nose out of Antrim business. And keep your trap shut!"

Figuring further argument was futile, Ryerson took a chair beside Kate and grabbed for her trembling hand. He put an arm around her, and she leaned her head on his shoulder without a word.

"Something will happen, Kate. Don't worry. They can't go through with this." He whispered it close to her ear.

Mort strolled back in, shaking his head. "Those fellers got the stage hitched finally. Judas Priest, even that driver didn't know straight up about harnessin' a team! He had the traces all bass-ackwards and I don't know what. No wonder the damned thing is always late!"

"They fixin' to go, Mort?" Mitch asked.

"The driver's climbing up on the box."

From outside, Ryerson heard the coaxing words to the team, heard the hooves digging in, the creak and squeak of the coach, the bird song of harness leathers being reefed against, and finally the rattle as it got under way across the uneven, rutted yard.

The Antrims hardly waited until the stage was out of hearing.

"Hey, you, big fella," Mitch roared at Bonner as though he was hard of hearing. "It's high time for you to get on outside. We're gonna take a walk down to them trees behind the shithouse."

Bonner looked up at Mitch in a blank stare matching that of Myles. Ryerson almost gaped in shock. Bonner had lost contact with what was going on around him, and with it went his willingness to fight.

"Antrim!" Ryerson called. "For the last time—"

Mitch swung the shotgun barrels around, aiming directly at Ryerson. "And for the last time, that's enough out of you, horse thief! Get over here with him." Ryerson stayed put. "Now, dammit!" Mitch screeched.

With resignation, Ryerson got up, leaned down and kissed Kate full on the lips for a long moment, and sauntered over to take his place beside Bonner. Something raged in his head that this wasn't happening, wouldn't happen, and couldn't happen.

"Myles!" Mitch roared. "Git down to them trees back of the barn. Get your wood together and git things ready. Hunt around for some rope. Mort! Tie Ryerson's hands. I don't want no funny business."

Myles leaped up from his chair, a drooly grin cutting his face open and showing darkened snags of teeth. His eyes were alight. "We—We git to do it now, Mitch?"

"I told you what to do, Myles. Now git about it, or you can sit here and wait and let me and Mort do it." Myles darted out the door. "The rest of you! Let's go. It's time."

The bright sunlight strung Ryerson's eyes after the long dark of night and the dimness of the cabin. They quickly adjusted.

"All right, Ryerson. You, too, Bonner," Mitch commanded. "Out behind the privy there. Let's go. The lady, too." Bonner started right out, but stumbling, still amazing Ryerson with his dumb acceptance of his approaching death.

Ryerson lagged, and Mitch nudged him between the shoulder blades with the shotgun muzzles. "Get a move on, outlander, or get it right here and now." Ryerson had seen that Mitch had both hammers cocked; he meant business.

With Mitch's rude shove, Ryerson stumbled across the dirt yard and headed down to the grove. All this couldn't be happening, he told himself. It was all a joke. It had to be. In a minute the Antrims would start cackling and tell him the laugh was on him.

Behind him Mort Antrim urged a sagging Kate along by the arm. She, too, was too numb with emotional strain and shock to realize what was happening, her mind hardly on the work of her feet.

In the center of the trees, in an open space, Myles Antrim had three long ropes tossed over sturdy limbs. He hustled around dragging in branches and dead limbs and breaking them into fire lengths with his feet or knees, or cracking big ones against tree trunks. The dimwit Antrim had, as he promised Mitch, gotten busy.

"Okay, hold it right here," Mitch commanded, an expectation in his voice like a preacher giving the invocation. "This is what we come for. Bonner goes first. We gonna make a day of this. Mort, you and Myles remember while we're doin' this what we found that was left of your brother and his wife, and what we got here is him that done it, and them that got in our way." He grabbed for Bonner's tied wrists, his voice turning ugly. "Come on here, you. You're first!"

He dragged the uncomprehending Bonner to one of the ropes. Bonner only whimpered softly like a scolded child. Mitch knelt and tied the trailing end of one dangling rope tight around Bonner's ankles. "All right, Mort and Myles. Up he goes!"

Bonner seemed oblivious to what was happening until Mort and Myles reefed on their end of the rope, pulling Bonner off his feet to topple heavily against the ground. In a moment he skidded along as the rope went taut, his straightened legs pointing skyward. The Antrim twins strained to hoist his heavy weight. "Christ, he's heavier than the first one was." Mort grunted. "Like a damned side of beef."

As Bonner's shoulders dragged free of the ground, his voice returned in a whiny kind of wail that grew in intensity until he screamed a wordless shriek of hysteria. The shrillness of his screech tore into Ryerson's ears, and he wanted to reach up and cover them to stifle the sound; his tied hands rendered him powerless.

"Shut up, gawdamn you!" Mitch screamed. "Shut up! Take it like your partner did, like a man!" Bonner continued to roar and struggle and writhe, hanging upside down. Bonner had turned powerful as a wounded bear against the death he now knew as imminent.

The dangling man's face was swollen and purple with the exertion and the blood rushing to it; it was inches from the ground. Mitch stepped to Bonner and, kicking him in the head, knocked him senseless. The shrill bellowing ceased instantly. Bonner dropped limp as a sack of suspended grain after having tried to grope for his secured ankles.

"Damn him! He better come to when his murderin' head starts to cook!" Mitch screamed in his blood lust. "I want to see this bastard squirm!"

A feverish, maddened excitement consumed the Antrims as they made their final preparations. Kate hung on Ryerson's shoulders, burying her head against his arm, wracked with terrorized convulsions. Much as Ryerson was compelled to take her in his arms to console her, he could hardly raise his tightly tied wrists above chest level. He coldly witnessed the Antrims as they got ready for Bonner's long execution. Suddenly he realized that all of his options had vanished. He thought of yelling again in protest, but knew it would only bring him a blow to the head that would knock him senseless, or a charge from one of the barrels of Mitch Antrim's scattergun, loaded and cocked.

"Myles!" Mitch ordered, an insane shrillness rising in his voice. "The wood—"

"I—I git to built tha fa'r," Myles stammered, dragging in his firewood lengths and piling them under Bonner's unconscious head.

"Mort, snub the end of that rope good to the tree, hear? He's up high enough. Get over here and watch these two. Ryerson still might try some funny stuff."

Mort had looped several lengths of rope around the tree to hold it, and now tied the free end holding Bonner suspended and turned to step close to Mitch. Behind him from the dense thicket, Ryerson flinched in surprise with the sharp, cracking explosion of a rifle.

Hit square in the chest, Mitch Antrim recoiled, his legs folding. He ingloriously plunked heavily to his rump, and his shotgun slid from his grip, dropping at an angle. The butt thudded heavily against the hard ground, jarring loose both cocked hammers.

A shock wave of concussion throbbed through the air around Ryerson's head.

Mort, walking toward his brother, was taken full in the belly and groin by the blast, his pants turning to tatters and spouting blood and mangled flesh and intestine.

Mort staggered backward with the impact and then regained his balance and stood weaving, groping with his hands where his genitals used to be. He crossed both hands over the blood-spewing hole, trying to hold in something that was already gone. He stepped forward in ungainly, spread-legged steps, his face drained, his eyes wide in disbelief.

"Mitch," Mort cried in a soft whine. "Whydja . . . ?" Mort dropped to his knees, still holding his blood-jellied groin. He knelt a long moment and pitched, face forward, still holding himself with blood-drenched hands.

Mitch had rolled over and lay dead a few feet from his dying brother.

Near the unconscious dangling hulk that was Lacey Bonner, Myles Antrim stood with two sticks of wood, as wide-eyed as Mort had been, his mouth agape and his tongue lazily circling his lips. A long, low animal whine slowly oozed from the astonished opening in his face.

His slow pace spelling out his agony, Tom Moon Dog limped painfully from behind a tree, gingerly favoring his swollen leg, the Winchester still at the ready, even though the contest with the Antrims was over.

In the suddenness of the event, Kate Folsom had raised her head from Ryerson's shoulder. "Tom!" she gasped.

Tom's face was a frozen mask of agony, drained of its magnificent Apache color from the monumental exertion of dragging his tormented body and tortured leg down from the cabin. Still he managed a grin at Ryerson, whose heart felt ready to burst. It's over, Ryerson's racing mind shouted, glory hallelujah, it's over! We made it!

Moon Dog's grin broke into a broad smile, despite his pain. "It's a good thing I remembered I had cartridges in my room. My empty rifle was still on my horse right by the door," he started, his voice tight with pain, but still sounding triumphant. "They . . . I realized the truth, Cole, when they finally hurt me so much I had to tell them how I got crippled. I knew then you couldn't have done it. It was as you said. You have too much honor to lie. But I told them of my hate, anyway. It was convenient ... and easy to say. I've lived with it so long. Too long. But it made them forget me."

"So you'd be able to do this," Ryerson said weakly.

"So I could do this."

"Well, Moon Dog, you're a damned good shot ... up close."

Ryerson couldn't hold back his own broad smile of total relief. He shoved out his restrained wrists. "Your knife's still tucked in my boot top, Tom. Would you do me a favor?"